The Rise of the African Empire

What if the German Empire fled to Tanganyika after WW1?

Rewriting History – 2024

Beware! Fun content ahead!

I have decided to prioritize entertainment over realism, so this book isn't supposed to be too realistic, although it's heavily inspired by many historical events.

Some events are altered to benefit the narrative and this fictional world, but this allows us for the most entertaining scenario I managed to come up with.

If I do something that is as realistic as possible, we will just get the historical scenario, with a defeat for the German Empire and the Kaiser. Where is the fun in that, where's the underdog story? If you're looking for something realistic, this is NOT it! You can just read a plain old history book instead. If you're looking for something entertaining, with a lot of historical content, this is the best book you can pick up to serve you that!

If you're still reading, this book is for you!

Table of Contents

Why are we here, just to suffer? 3
The Kaiser? Never heard of him! 24
Veni, Vidi, Vici 30
Austrian rules Germany? This is fine! 45
Abyssinia or Ethiopia? Neither! 50
In dire need of a Naval Admiral… 58
Crisis, crisis, crisis! 71
You want a battle, here's a war! 82
Intervene and steal or help and take! 115
What's the equivalent of the Eiffel Tower in Germany? 138
Life is good! I feel good! 144
Revolution! 149

Why are we here, just to suffer?

- I remember back in the day going to the market in the town's center, and it just... there were a lot of choices back then. I try to keep an open mind and be thankful for what I've got, but I still miss the past. Right now, I struggle to integrate into these new conditions, as I'm surrounded by people, I'm unused to. It's true, I have seen all kinds of shit! I used to fight for the Kaiser, and I personally commanded the 5th army of the German Empire. I just feel like all of this is unfair, and uhh... do you have a light?
- In the drawer beneath the documents, you should find one box. I brought these personally, but I don't find a lot of these nowadays.

(lights a cigar)

(puffs)

(silence)

- So, uhm... where was I Oh wait, have you ever read Romeo and Juliet?
- No sir, I don't think I have.
- It's a great book, or so I heard, what a shame it was written by a Brit!

(laughter)

- But yeah, where was I already forgot what I was telling you.
- Something about the war being unfair.
- Damn right! - slams the table - in October 1914 I said in an interview, in perfect English I might add. It went along the lines of This is the most stupid and unnecessary war of modern times. It is a war not wanted by Germany, but it was forced on us. We were so effectively prepared to defend ourselves that it's being used as an argument to convince the world that we desired conflict." I don't know about you, but I miss home, and I'm a grown man. Look Karl, can I ask you something.
- Uhh, what, do you want me to marry you?

(laughter)

- Of course, not you idiot. I want you to go to the market and buy something special for tomorrow, it's a big day.
- Something to smoke?
- Preferably.
- Will see you at noon, good luck!
- Thanks, Karl!

20 years earlier

(turns on radio)

"The German Empire has officially been captured! Rejoice everyone, the war is officially over! Let this lead to a better version of Europe, without any conflict."

- This is all I hear and read in the newspapers, what a heavy blunder that must be. Our people are going to regret that deeply and will suffer in the coming years.
- Versailles ain't that bad, could be worse.
- No, no, no, that's the problem with you! Germany should have won! Anything that is not a victory is complete humiliation of our proud nation! We should continue fighting, let us not give up, we have a chance. The entente has barely entered mainland Germany, we can focus on a war of attrition!
- Sir please, it's unnecessary for more German lives to be wasted on such a pointless war, we lost, sire.
- You're wrong - throws glass at the floor, which breaks - We can still win! The German people are strong and can endure another million casualties, but not the losses at Versailles! We can just defend our lines and make it so costly for them to reach Berlin that it's not worth it, so they will simply give up!
- But in that case, I don't see us winning either way - says an unknown army general who just entered the room - In my humble opinion what you're suggesting won't work out. I see 2 scenarios playing out, in the first, the enemy doesn't reach Berlin, but takes the Rhineland and much of our industry, so we will be the ones starving into submission. The

other option is that the enemy simply takes the Rhineland and doesn't care to push to Berlin, which won't benefit us. The war is lost, I suggest accepting the terms and trying it out again in the next one. I'm sorry.
- No, you're fired! This cannot be like that! What you're suggesting has no truth to that, you're too old to know any better!
- Look, you're like a son to me, I would never lie to you! Listen to me, we need to try in the next war!
- We cannot, as the Empire is going to be abolished, me and my father won't rule Germany after we sign it, the people will! You might be there to help them, but I cannot lead them to victory!
- How about Tanganyika?
- What about that place?
- It's still not conquered, and the entente lacks the resources to do so. It looks to be safe, for now.
- So, who cares about that colony, which just takes resources away from the mainland, rather than producing and sending it here!
- It can become your biggest asset, sire, but only if you're smart about it! Listen, you can go there and continue the German Empire's legacy. You better hope that France and Britain end up at war with the new Germany, so you can aid them and hopefully secure the throne!
- You're suggesting a government in exile? To give up all we have right now.
- I believe it's your only choice and if I were you, I would do that.
- There is no way for us to get there, who would allow us, the British, of course not!
- The Dutch!

(silence fills the room)

- You have good relations with them, so they can take you to Tanganyika. They can even justify that they're going to the East Indies and drop you off on the way there, nobody's going to know.
- Look, I want to go out for some fresh air, I need to clear my head.
- I won't be here long, I need to go and see your father, think about it, tomorrow I will visit you at 7, hope you have your mind ready!

(door opens and closes)

"I can't believe I'm about to betray my people. I'm not a coward, but running away, I cannot do that but is it really running if I plan, and even insist on returning I guess not!

The weather is nice for a time such late in the year. The snow feels nice. That said, if we really do what Ferdinand suggested, we need to move to Africa. I don't know a lot, haven't been there, but I met soldiers who were stationed there. They said it's too hot and it's never snowing, I really cannot imagine that.

What am I thinking about, the snow isn't what I'll miss the most, it's what I have here - bangs at chest - it's about where I'm standing right now, it's all about the motherland!

Suppose continuing the war is not possible, going into exile might be my best choice right now. The Dutch will aid us, and hundreds of thousands of loyalists would join us in this endeavor. We can do something in the future, we mustn't lose our legitimacy.

What's the population of German East Africa, do I know I don't!"

(Walks inside, heads down the staircase, goes to a door and knocks on it, the door opens)

- Ah Friedrich, what brought you here?
- I want you to tell me about something, but don't let anyone know I was here, right!
- Right...
- Do you have a population map around here?
- What are you looking for exactly?
- Something about the colonies.
- Oh, forget about them, we will lose them once your father signs the peace treaty.
- No, no, I mean it, show me.
- Go to your right, no wait, to my right, then continue and aha, there. Take this bunch of paper, there you will find everything you will need! I have no need for that, we will lose them either way.
- You never disappoint Karl, good night!

\- Goodnight to you too, sir!

"I wonder how many people live there, is there any industry or arms factories. It's going to take me all night to figure it out. It's alright, it's just me and my thoughts, with hopefully no other disseminations."

(sits in chair)

(lights matches)

(puffs cigar)

"7,7 million in 1912, who counted all of these people? Anyways, this can work. There can be around 8 million right now, and if another million loyalists flee, we can secure our place, not bad.

Still, the enemy can send an army of 500,000 soldiers our way, we cannot hope to both rule over the natives and to secure a victory. I think that we should integrate them, making them join the army and defend their freedo… no wait, am I stupid? Who would dare to do that? Well, desperate times do require desperate measures. We can also promise them independence once we return, so they will fight to defend us.

Tanganyika will become a stronghold that wouldn't fall to the enemy! This is our only chance! But the British won't let go, there is a high chance they blockade us, so they can starve us into submission. Tanganyika is by far not self-sufficient."

(pours liquid into glass)

"This… it can work! I need to think about it carefully, so I can lead the people to a better life, cannot figure it out on the go! Now, how would the enemy respond? The British want this land dearly, as it's important for them to build this damn railroad. They won't let us have it without a fight!

We can respond to an army of 500,000 and if we hold them at bay, the terrain is favorable for that, they can drop out of the war. Let's hope my father doesn't become Napoleon after he returned from that island, what was it called? Uh, forget about it."

(pours liquid into glass)

(relights cigar)

"Our soldiers cannot hope to hold, but what about the natives?"

(exhales cigar smoke)

"Suppose we give them freedom and promise to leave... Hmm... They can fight for us with their damn lives. So, if Britain conquers them so they can build their railroad, the people will resist! They have already seen what it's like to be free under Germany. They will resist the Brits if they know what's going to happen. We can use this! This can work."

(inhales and exhales cigar smoke)

"What about guns? We don't have one for everyone... We can either purchase or..."

(knocks on door)

- Ja?

(door opens)

- I was surprised you're not asleep, but I could smell that cigar from a mile away, so I decided to check in on you.
- What do you want?

(drops the ash from the cigar)

- Have you read the treaty?
- You mean Weimar becoming the new Berlin? This is so funny! I swear they chose this place just to annoy us, they cannot be serious! I hate it! This is so unfair and we're not the ones who asked for this w...
- I know, I know. Look, the war is over, get some rest! Hey, what are you looking at?
- Suppose there is a plan B and not all is lost?
- I'm all ears.
- Don't worry about that, tomorrow at 7 I will tell you.
- So, you don't know, hah?

(pours liquid into glass)

- Not yet, but I'm onto something.
- Don't get your hopes up, we lost, this is it.

(door opens and closes)

"So, he wants to live in the Netherlands, huh? The Dutch, they're good friends, how can we use that? Wait, the treaty... it sends shivers down my spine just thinking about it, but... We can work with that. Ferdinand told me earlier to hope that France and Britain end up at war with the new Germany, so we can join from East Africa and secure our homeland! But how is that possible, even if something were to happen, the conflict would be soon over."

(knocks down the glass, it hits the floor and shatters into a thousand pieces)

- Damn it! – slams the table.

(stands up and reaches for another glass, pours liquid into said glass, relights cigar)

"Where was I... think... think... the war. We lost, the new Germany would also lose, but it won't take them 4 years, I give them 4 months at best, they have no allies. This won't be a challenge for the enemy, they need a challenge, so they can rely on our support, which would allow us to return. We need to be the deciding factor."

(puffs on cigar)

"Need to make Germany weaker on purpose, so there is a communist revolution. They can ally with the Russians! Aha!" – slams table. – "This should work! We still have control over Germany, so we can ruin it. We need ripe conditions for a communist revolution! What made Russia go communist? They lost the war, we have that! The people were starving... we can assure that. They had a provisional government which failed, we can set conditions up for the Weimar Republic to fail! We can also starve the people and promote Karl Marx's ideology, while we're still in power. This makes sense, this way, Germany will not be defeated so easily by the enemy. A war should break out between the new Germany, together with the Russians, who would fight against France and Britain. The odds are even, so we can join to tip the scale. All works out in our favor; we need to ruin Germany on purpose so we can get power later!"

(pours liquid into glass)

"But the communists did fail a couple of months ago. The Bavarian Soviet Republic had their chance but were brutally put down by the Freikorps. These troops cannot be trusted! They were supposed to protect the Kaiser but are protecting the interests of the new Germany! This doesn't mean that we cannot use them for our interests! Wolfgang Kapp can be our greatest asset! We can push for him to do something. No matter what, we should destabilize the Weimar Government as much as possible, we don't care if the coup succeeds or not! This gives me relief."

(finishes drinking from the glass)

"I have a solid plan, this can work, we can take back Germany! I should rest now, this will work, this is solid!"

(shuts off lights)

...

- Good morning Fridrick!
- Hello, Karl!
- I see you're doing better today. Did you have any use of the papers you took yesterday?
- I did, thank you! Listen, do you know where I can find my father?
- Uhm... last time I saw him he went by that lake, won't go anywhere too far I bet!

(walks towards the lake and approaches a man, sitting on a bench)

- Good morning, father.
- Glad to see you've had a good night's sleep. What were you doing yesterday that late?
- I don't know, what were you?

(taps on shoulder)

- Listen, father, I have an idea.
- So, you finally came up with something? Tell me!
- We go to German East Africa.
- Tanganyika?

(man erupts in laughing)

- Is this what you thought of? Hahaha!
- Listen, father, I spoke with Ferdinand, this is his suggestion, I just thought about it.
- Well, if Ferdinand came up with that, I assume that it's something smart. Tell me more. – throws rock at the pond.
- It still hasn't capitulated; we can go there and establish a government in exile. Then, we wait for France and Britain to go to war with Germany again, which should happen in a couple of years, then we support them and take back our homeland.
- Wait, breathe. You're speaking too much!
- This can work!
- And why would Germany go to war with France and Britain in a few years?
- They won't! France and Britain would go to war against them.
- How?
- We still have power over Germany, we can make Versailles even harsher on the Germans. This should provoke a communist revolution.
- But the last few failed? What's so different now?
- Russia, I bet would support the German communists! We have power over the treaty, let's make it harsher! You know why Russia dropped out of the war, right?
- Um... let me guess... poverty, low morale, failure of the provisional government... and yeah, losing the great war...
- We can ensure that happens to our people too! They will get radicalized and hate the French and the British for these harsh terms, ensuring a successful communist revolution. Then this new Germany would ally with Russia, so they would end up fighting France and Britain soon. The

scales are even I would say. We can intervene from German East Africa and tip the scales! This will allow us to take back our homeland!
- Sounds more exciting than house arrest in the Netherlands I will admit, it can work. But how do we get there, how do we rule the country, there is so much to consider.
- I already considered it, read this.

(hands pieces of paper, some marked with ink)

(long silence)

(man goes by the 2 gentlemen sitting at the table)

(man throws rock at the pond)

- Makes sense… but why do you need Wolfgang Kapp?
- We don't, he will just destabilize Germany more, most likely he won't succeed. We will just use him and tell him to go ahead, he has radicalized soldiers and influence among them.
- Let's see how this would play out. Are you doing it tomorrow?
- I think so, you need to write a letter.
- I will.
- Father, I will head out to see how would come with us in East Africa, I need to make a list.
- Go on.
- Albright, tschüss.
- Tschüss.

12 hours later

(people cheering)

(loud room)

- Listen, do you have a minute?

(man puts down cigar)

- I'm all ears.

- Look, I thought about what you told me. We should insist on Versailles being harsher. Tomorrow I will send a diplomat who will try to anger the Entente, which would hopefully result in a harsher treaty.
- Let's move to somewhere quieter, follow me!

(chairs move, door opens and closes)

- What are you hoping to achieve with that?
- The easiest way to radicalize our population is to give France an occupation zone over Germany, doesn't have to be big, just something that would a thorn in the sight of the people. The Saarland makes the most sense, we give them that and all of Germany is going to be mad! Tomorrow our delegate would do such a poor job that the Entente would request even more.
- We can also force the New Germany, or the Entente to force the New Germany to give this damn land to Denmark. This should also help.
- Isn't the Polish corridor enough of a punishment?
- I don't think so!
- What about the coup? The one with Wolfgang Kapp?
- What's today?
- 12th of March, sire.
- The 13th is going to be a big day in German history if we act quickly. We have the army that fought in the Baltics ready, they're radicalized. We can cause more trouble in the New Germany. Let's give them all that they request, I will go and talk to the soldiers!
- Let me know if you need anything.
- Tomorrow is going to be a big day, I know that much!

(making a toast sound)

- Let's drink to that, no matter what happens, we will come out on top!

(doors opens and closes)

The next day

- Karl, do you have the report of the operation?

- Here you go sire, all is written in detail!

"In Berlin at around 10:00 pm. German soldiers stormed the city, having a swastika painted on their helmets. The Government has fled Berlin, as they knew of the upcoming unrest. The Weimar Government declared that everyone in Germany should go on strike. Communication in the whole of Germany is cut."

- Does this look promising?
- I'm afraid not, sire. The rebels in Berlin would get crushed over time, and without communication, no troops could be sent there in time to reinforce them.
- We should leave tonight then.
- I strongly agree. Do you want me to go with you right away, or join you later?
- Stay here for the time being, make sure that as many of the monarchist loyalists and members of the Freikorps learn of our hideout in East Africa and join us!
- Understood, tomorrow I will request a ship to wait for you at Rotterdam, you should take everyone with you.

(opens a glass bottle)

(closes it)

"I should take it with me, don't think I will find many of these in Africa. For that matter, I should take everything that I can. Need a whole other ship to carry all I need. Good thing that Karl is here, I will tell him what I need via letters, and he will give it to me.

Tomorrow... we're leaving this New Germany... God, I hope that I will return and save my people from their fate... God save Germany, and the Germans. Gott mit uns!"

(turns of the lights)

The next day

"I really cannot get out of bed, and I have been awake for more than an hour. I feel sick, but I know I'm not. This is not because of the heavy drinking either, I know what it feels like. There is just this unsettling feeling in my stomach and throat. I can't believe what I'm about to do, but this is for the best of the German people! I must get up, the train is waiting for me."

- Guten Morgen, your Majesty, breakfast is ready!
- I'm not interested, Danke!

(walks away and waits for the train)

- You came in early?
- I couldn't really sleep, then I couldn't get out of bed.
- I understand, but you know why we're doing this, right?
- Yes, I'm ready!
- Look! The train is here! Ready to board? Hah, like we have a choice! Get in, son.

(man kneels to the ground and kisses it)

(whispers)

- God, save Germany!

Hours later

(writes on paper)

"I didn't want to do this, but all I wish for is a strong Germany! The New Germany will be too unsuccessful and soon they will collapse, hopefully to a communist revolution. I really hope to return in the coming years. I, the Crown Prince of Germany, will save the German people from their fate, nobody else can!

We have secured that this new Germany is going to be weaker. We pushed for harsher terms. If it wasn't for our involvement, the occupation of the Saarland, giving southern Schleswig to Denmark, and the army limit, would most probably never happen. We made it! The conditions are ripe for a communist takeover, then we will return from exile, then we will be victorious! Gott mit uns!"

About a month later

(horn of a lighthouse)

- We're here! We made it! Your Majesty, come and see! This is our new home!

(man opens door, exits)

(follows the woman)

(goes to the dock of the ship)

- Which island is this, Capitan?
- Comoros, they're French.

(spits into the water)

- Pesky French, they're allowed to have this, but we aren't!

(silence)

- How close are we to docking?
- Docking? Hahaha! You have no idea what we're doing. We will stop in Lindi, there is no port there! We cannot dock in Der Es Salaam, it's close to Zanzibar, which is British, they will notice. Your Majesty, you're all encircled in this place, the French and British are to each side you look, better hope that they don't find you! Anyways, we will arrive in 4 hours, Heinrich Schnee is instructed to build a temporary dock there, we shall see.

(silence)

- Your majesty, we're in French territorial waters. I suggest you hide for the time being, if they find you, we will have a lot of problems.

(man walks back to his cabin)

"God, what is this place? We cannot even dock properly!"

(throws glass at the wall, it breaks)

"Keep it cool, we still haven't arrived, all should be good!"

4 hours later

(loud bang on door)

(French speaking)

(mumbling, whispers)

(another loud bang)

"French? What is going on?"

(French loud speaking through the door)

"I will hide under my bed. God save me!"

(door opens)

(footsteps)

(mumbling)

"They're two, and I think one has a rifle. Let me not make any noise…"

(heavy breathing)

(door closes)

30 minutes later

(door opens)

- Your Majesty, it's me! Haha, we escaped! Show yourself, it's safe!

"Is that so? Let me see… He's alone… There goes nothing!"

(man rolls out from under the bed)

- Your Majesty, you have packed so much tobacco and alcohol that I managed to convince the French patrol that I'm going to sell it in the East Indies, haha! What a lucky day!
- Thank God!
- Prepare to step out of this damn boat, we will arrive shortly.

"Finally… I hope this was worth it, haven't felt worse in years, or maybe… hmm… I don't think I've felt this bad, ever. Even during the war. The trenches were more comfortable I think."

(lighthouse horn intensifies)

- We're close – shouts the Capitan.

Hours later

(man writes on paper)

"We made it safely… Right now, I'm in a wooden hut and I must admit, it's worse than the trenches. Here it's so hot, I have never experienced it in my life. The people are so different, they're shorter, they're darker. Nobody speaks German here, except the whites. I thought this was part of Germany… We should change that!"

(man knocks on door)

(man walks to the door, opens it)

- Your Majesty, I am Heinrich Schnee, the Governor of German East Africa, glad to see you made it safely!

(shakes hand)

- Let me take you on a tour around the place, we need to find you a residence. Also, apologies for the lack of a loud celebration of your arrival, being 90 kilometers from a British territory and making such a noise isn't a wise thing to do!

- I'm glad you thought about that!
- Your Majesty, get on the horse, I hope you know how to get your way around, there will be a lot of traveling! I want to show you around the region, your luggage will follow you.

(both men get on a horseback)

- Wait, your Majesty, take this.

(man hands a hat to another man)

- You will need this, here it gets too hot sometimes. Now is especially dry.
- I have a couple of questions that have bothered me ever since I boarded that damn ship, but I had nobody to ask.

(man lights a cigarette)

- I can answer, your Majesty. Do you want one?

(hands a pack of cigarettes)

(both men light a cigarette)

- So, I wanted to ask you why we simply don't dock in Der Es Salaam, is all of this hiding necessarily?
- I'm afraid it is, your Majesty. Let me tell you a story. Do you know who is Khalid bin Barghash?
- Not a German, I know that much!
- Ha! He was neither a Brit too! This story may interest you. Hermann Wissmann, I bet you have heard of this name.

(man nods head)

- When he was Imperial Governor of German East Africa, something really interesting happened. The British had a conflict with Zanzibar, so they invaded them.
- How come?
- This guy I mentioned earlier, Khalid bin Barghash wanted to take the throne due to succession crisis or whatever. He barricaded himself in the palace and the British bombed it into submission. Khalid bin

Barghash disappeared and 500 of his loyalists were dead. Here comes the funny part, he took refuge in the German Ambassy in Zanzibar.
- Wait, what year is that.
- 1896.

(man nods head)

- So, I'm telling you all this, just so you know that Der Es Salaam is not a safe place to be. On the 3rd of September 1916 the British occupied Der Es Salaam, and believe it or not, after exactly 20 years of hiding, they found Khalid bin Barghash and send him to Saint Helena.

(both men stop)

- Did I hear you correctly? Saint Helena?
- You did, your Majesty, the same island where Napoleon Bonaparte was exiled, indeed.

"God damn it! Is this my future if I get discovered?"

- This is why Der Es Salaam is not a safe place, your Majesty. We need to travel inland, I suggest establishing a settlement around Dodoma, it's in the middle of the country. Do you know what Dodoma means in Bulgarian?
- I may know some languages, but Bulgarian is not one of them.

(both men laugh)

- It means "next to home", which is quite fitting, don't you think?
- What a coincidence! But is it safe?
- Your Majesty, I believe it's the safest place in all of German East Africa.
- How come?
- Lindi, the town you just arrived in was occupied by Britain in September 1916. Just 100 kilometers from that is the town of Mahiwa, which fell in October 1917.
- A year's difference.

(man points a finger at his colleague)

- Spot on! The more inland you go, the later the British captured it. Even if the worst happens and Britian and France invade, it will take them years to reach you, given that you have enough soldiers to hold the lines.

(man lights another cigar)

- Your Majesty, I said that Dodoma is the safest, because during the war, it never fell, one of the few cities I'm aware of that didn't.
- How come?
- It's too far from any supply lines, warfare in Africa is not the same as in Europe, as one German famously shouted, it's all about supply! It just makes it really difficult to supply tens of thousands of troops, hundreds of kilometers away, into enemy territory. Dodoma is as safe as it gets. This is if we go there. You will like it, there are 2 lakes, from which we will get fresh water, so we can survive, but the enemy won't reach us!
- How far away is this?
- From Lindi to Dodoma it's exactly 600 kilometers, on horseback, we should be there in a week, give or take. Let me tell you, you're one lucky runaway. Halfway through the journey is the town of Kitadu, there we can board a train to Dodoma.
- A train?
- Correct, your majesty. We have railroad tracks stretching all the way from lake Tanganyika to the Indian ocean, so from one side of the country to the other. We also have a railroad connection from the north to the east. Dodoma is in the middle of all that, which would make German East Africa really easy to govern from there and really hard to conquer.
- You have done your research, Schnee, I'm proud of you!
- Everything for Kaiser! Long live Kaiser!

(both men laugh)

- So it's 600 kilometers to Dodoma and halfway through we will catch a train, so it's 300 kilometers on horseback?
- Give or take, yes! We should be in Dodoma in 5 or 6 days.
- That's such a journey...

- It could have been worse, you could have gone to Tanga, which fell months after the start of the war. There your fate would have been sealed for sure. Remember, if it's hard for you, it's also hard for the enemy! Who will come looking for the Kaiser in the middle of nowhere?

(both men laugh)

A couple of days later

(man writes on paper)

"Last time I was on a train was so long ago, and it was on the way to Rotterdam where I boarded this damn ship. The journey across East Africa gives me hope that nobody would dare to look for me here. The terrain is very easy to defend, we just need the manpower. This should be as simple as giving the natives freedom. Heard that they're doing well in Ethiopia by doing this.

Oh, regarding the journey. I was told there is many dangerous wild animals, but I didn't see any. I saw a giraffe - this one impressed me. The long neck must mean something, nature wouldn't create it out of nowhere. It can be a disadvantage, but I think that it's the biggest asset of the animal. The food takes longer to travel from the mouth to the stomach and for the brain signals to reach the body. This may be the reason why this animal is so slow.

With this long neck I saw it reach fruits that other animals simply couldn't. This is no disadvantage, but something clever by nature. I want to become like a giraffe, I must think like a giraffe. I must discover my unfair advantage. Everybody has one, but if they don't use it, they perish. If the giraffe eats only low hanging fruits that other animals can reach, it will starve to death, as it's too slow. Somebody would steal the fruit beneath its nose.

So, what is my unfair advantage? I don't know, but I must discover it, or I will perish. Will figure it out once I settle in Dodoma."

The Kaiser? Never heard of him!

"Ladies and Gentlemen of the Weimar Republic, it has come to my knowledge that the Kaiser, his family, many loyal army generals and soldiers have fled!

The Kaiser was in house arrest in the Netherlands, but he seems to have escaped. We don't know where he is, and the Dutch don't know either."

(crowd is dissatisfied)

- Traitor of the people!
- Kaiser has abandoned us!
- No! The Kaiser will save us!
- No!

(the crowd erupts in action)

(people start hitting each other)

(the army intervenes)

(people get dispersed)

(man lights cigar)

- Do you really think that Kaiser has abandoned us?
- I don't think so...

(man puffs on cigar)

- And why is that?
- Why else would he take the army generals and soldiers with him? If were to abandon us, he would have been left alone. He must be planning something.
- Whatever it is, I support him. This New Germany is unacceptable... Listen Jacob, I want to go home, will talk to you tomorrow.
- Why tomorrow? Are you going to work?
- I think so.

- Ha! You're so naive! Why would you do that, you will get your salary either way. You going to work would only benefit the damn French! Stay at home and collect your paycheck.
- We will see, will see you around Jacob.
- Gute Nacht, Hans.

(man waves goodbye)

An unknown amount of time later

"I am a simple person, but I did wish for riches. I have always worked my ass of and I don't know what to do now that I'm not supposed to go to work. The government has told me, Hans, stay at home, don't work for the French occupiers. Hans, do this, do that.

I'm tired of that. I did wish to be a millionaire, but not like that. I don't know what is happening in this New Germany, but the conditions are brutal. I cannot believe that on a simple coin it would say 5,000,000 marks. Can you imagine that? 5 million on a simple plain brass coin? This is insanity, this is not normal. Back in my day, no, 5 years ago, 1 Deutscher Mark contained 5 grams of silver exactly. Now? 5 million contain 0 grams of silver.

I guess I should watch out what I wish for, shouldn't have wished for money, but for assets instead, nobody can take that away from you.

Kaiser, please save me!"

(man climbs on chair)

(puts rope around his neck)

(drops down)

The next day

- Guten Morgen Hans, are you free for a beer?

(silence)

- What's up? You don't want to talk with your best friend? Listen Hans, I'm sorry if I said something yesterday, I barely went home last night.

(man shows his neck)

(other man gasps)

- Listen… I don't know why you would do such a thing… There is something you wish for that you can achieve, right? So why don't you work towards that?
- I want Kaiser to return and fix this damn country!
- Go and find him then!
- Jacob!
- No, I'm serious. This will keep you busy! You will have a goal you cannot reach, but at least you won't do such stupid stuff.
- You know what, you're right, I will find the Kaiser! I gotta go!

(man runs away)

"The Kaiser didn't abandon us, I'm sure of that! I think he escaped, but not to abandon us! We will figure out soon. Let me go to work, I don't know what else to do, I'm going insane I feel it!"

(man arrives at a factory)

- Hey, what are you doing here? We're closed!
- I work here! Then why would you come here? Don't you know, the government will pay you either way, so go and enjoy life.
- Enjoy life you say, huh?

(shows his scar on the neck)

- Listen, I want to ask you something. Do you know what happened to Kaiser?
- This guy? He's the reason why we're in this situation right now! I hope he is dead.
- No!

(silence)

- He will save this country! Don't you remember the time before the war. We were on top of the world! Now... now we have nothing! How many millions of marks does a loaf of bread cost now, and how much did it cost when Kaiser ruled us?
- Who cares? How many millions was your salary during the Kaiser and right now? It's all the same, you just cannot see it! I'm tired of all these loyalists of th...

(man stabs the other man)

- This is for Kaiser!

(man spits on the ground)

"What... what did I just do? No... no... I must escape, cannot be closed up. I need to find Jacob and tell him what happened. Do I? Nobody should know, right? If I tell somebody, I risk getting shot. I'm innocent... Innocent people are getting shot in the New Germany, however. God, Kaiser, save me, save Germany!"

Berlin is exactly 6,860 kilometers away from Dodoma.

"The German Empire, German East Africa, land of the free, who would have guessed that? Here, the natives rule themselves and we taught them the ways of European life. Work-life balance was introduced, and the cities are industrialized. Although nobody here has finished university, the people are learning, as the whites are sharing their knowledge. The German Empire is a heaven on Earth!"

- This sounds good! I like how we're portrayed!
- Your Majesty, your reforms are working out, while they were unpopular among the Generals, for now it works.
- This is until the natives decide that they don't want us here.
- But you did promise them freedom after we reclaim Germany, right, sire?

- Correct, Karl, but who knows... Maybe they won't rise against us, after all they would be educated like Europeans, who didn't rise against us. You know what I'm missing the most?
- What, sire?
- Everything being in German. While here we have most things in German, many villages are in their native language, which I struggle to pronounce. Can't we just change some names to something in German? For example, Dodoma can become Neu Berlin, or Neu Germania.
- Haha! You might as well call Dodoma as "Friedrich Wilhelm Victor August Ernst, Crown Prince of Germany lives here"

(laugher among both men)

- What matters is that they're joining the military on mass. 500,000 people have enlisted in only 6 months of us being here.

"500,000. This is a lot! I predicted that if the former Entente of France and Britain would tried to fight us, they would ammas a similar army size at most. We're now even, but we're lacking equipment and training, so we're not even, yet."

- What about the weapons situation, we need to figure something out.
- Your Majesty, if you're open to work with the Soviet Union, we can purchase many outdated weapons from them, for really cheap too! They just finished fighting their civil war, so they need money to recover, and we need guns to protect ourselves.
- Do we have any other alternatives, Karl?
- Not really. We can work with Japan, but the prices per unit is at least triple than the one of the Soviets. Spain is also a good option, but they're not willing to sell us too much, so we're limited on the quantity we can purchase. There's not a lot of options, working with the Soviets can work, after all, the idea is that they ally with the New Germany and fight France and Britain. Us purchasing Soviet equipment would aid in that.
- What you're saying fundamentally makes sense, but I don't like it. Karl, let me think about this for a bit.
- Of course, sire, Gute Nacht.
- Tschüss!

(door opens, door closes)

Veni, Vidi, Vici

- Your Majesty, you may be interested to find out what just happened in the Kingdom of Italy.

(man hands newspaper)

"King Victor Emmanuel III refused to declare a state of emergency and transferred power to the Fascists.

Faced with mounting pressure and fearing the possibility of civil conflict, the government ultimately chose not to confront the Fascists. Instead, King Victor Emmanuel III, under advice from his ministers, invited Mussolini to form a new government. Mussolini was appointed Prime Minister on October 29, 1922.

The characteristics of the Italian fascists are as follows:

Authoritarianism - Strong, centralized state led by a single leader or dictator.

Nationalism: Promoting the idea of a unified and powerful Italian state.

Totalitarianism: Total control over all aspects of society, including politics, the economy, culture, and education.

Militarism: Military strength and aggression, viewing war as a means of achieving national greatness and expansion.

Anti-Communism: Communism as a threat to national unity and stability."

- What do you think?
- I don't think we can work with these guys, this sounds extreme to me. Look at this, - man points at the newspaper - Anti-Communism, I wished that France and Britain were communist, then we can work with these guys.
- What about the guns?
- The guns?

- Weapons for the army, I mean, your Majesty. They could be willing to sell us equipment. If good relations are secured, despite the ideology, something can work out. They're colonial neighbors, or do we rather to work with France, Britain, or maybe Belgium.
- Portugal too...
- Yes, sire, also Portugal.
- You're right, Karl. We fought all of these countries, neither of which should be strengthened. Italy controls Somalia and Eritrea, we can trade. I want you to arrange a meeting with the Italian Duce, send our official congratulations for him becoming ruler of the Kingdom of Italy, and wish him all the best!
- On it, sire!

(door opens, door closes)

Days later

(map picks up newspaper)

"The year is 1923 and Europe is finally calm, with no more conflict. All of this started with Wilhelm II starting a world war, a war never seen before, fought on many continents! While Europe was 4 years at war and for another 5 at civil war and many conflicts, the Kaiser and the Crown Prince and living in heaven on earth in East Africa.

We, the British people, should make sure that the Kaiser and his family pay for all that chaos he caused to the continent for whole 9 years! German East Africa must fall and the Kaiser should be held accountable!"

- Father, what do you think about this?
- We must act quickly! This is their justification. We have people in London who will tell us if there is any mobilization, but there is a problem.
- What is it?
- Information will arrive a month after it has started. Perhaps they're already mobilizing, we just don't know it yet.

- We are ready to resist, but we're lacking equipment.
- In a war of attrition, we have a chance. Secure guns at all costs, at any price. They're looking for revenge!

(door opens, door closes)

(man bangs on door)

- Come inside!
- Karl, did you read the news?
- I did, and I expected to see you here! The Italian Duce is willing to meet you in Rome after about a month.
- This doesn't help us, we need guns urgently!
- You can go and ask him personally. If you depart right now, you will arrive sooner, I will let him know of your journey.
- I'm risking leaving the country and then for Britain to declare war. I should stay here right now.
- Then, you will make the Duce wait, I have heard that he is impatient, this won't make a good impression.
- So, it's either to stay here and wait for war to be brought upon our Great Nation again, or to go to Italy and ask for help, but risk not being able to lead the country into this upcoming war. Neither of these options secure us good odds.

"Unfair advantage, what is mine? Have I found it yet? I don't think so! Normal animals eat food on the ground, but the giraffe uses its unfair advantage to reach fruit not available to other animals. If I were a giraffe, what would I do?"

- Let me go back to my room and think about it.
- Will be awaiting you, sire.

(door opens, door closes)

"Losers become losers by not being willing to lose. From where did I hear that? If I don't do something, I will still lose, but it's going to take me decades to lose. If I do the wrong thing, I will lose tomorrow. The only option for me is to win, but how?

Going to Italy can secure support, and with Italian help, the British may back down! I should risk it, my generals and people know how to hold the British advance, without my help. The Suez is closed to us, as Britian doesn't recognize our new state. We would need to travel all across Africa to get to Italy, and then... Gibraltar... Pesky British!"

(slams the table)

"They control all the chokepoints to the Mediterranean, going there is very tricky. Spain could allow us to dock, and then we travel by train from one side to the other... right. Then we board a ship again to reach Rome. This seems like my only option, but it's going to take months, longer than Karl predicted, and what I would have thought. This cannot work."

(man opens drawer)

(pulls out a box)

"The thing that helps me think and never disappoints. Hah! Who said that?"

(lights a cigar)

(inhales cigar smoke)

"I would be gone for at least 3 months if I go on this journey, which is plenty of time for Britian to invade and make sure I cannot return."

(exhales smoke)

"So, I have no options, which means that Britain also thinks I have no options. They would think I'm about to stay, so they want to capture me alive, or what is their goal? I should do what they least expect, so I should go to Italy, this is obvious. Drawing plans for 3 months is hard and close to impossible. Nobody can rule the Empire while I'm gone, and I cannot give instructions.

Is that my unfair advantage? Of knowing when to go and when to stay? I think so."

(pours liquid into glass)

"The Suez is closed, and they won't let us pass through Gibraltar. Right now, I realize how powerful Britain actually is, they control everything and if you disobey them, you will suffer. Too bad for them!"

(drinks all the content of the glass at once)

"The Suez is closed, but only for us. The Italians are a few hundred kilometers north of us. They pass through the Suez frequently to reach Italian East Africa, and then to go back to the mainland. If I sneak into one of these ships, I can make the journey really quickly, if I'm lucky it could take me less than a month to do that. This I feel like would catch the British off guard, resulting in our advantage. It can work, but I need to depart tomorrow. Hmm…"

(relights cigar)

(puffs on cigar)

"But if I go tomorrow, who will rule the Empire? I don't have time to give them instructions. They can maybe last a month without me, but what if Britain invades? The Empire will quickly fall, as they don't know what to do."

(silence)

"That's a risk I should take. If I don't, we will slowly lose. Without Italian support, we're doomed. Even if they agree to sell us weapons, I can take as much as I can carry in my ship with me and return to the Empire. We need some sort of an Italian aid urgently, or we will still lose, but it would take longer."

(inhales and exhales cigar)

"If I don't do something, it's not like I don't fail, I just fail long. The results of my failures are not seen tomorrow, but after months. Any mistake can be corrected, so I better act today, fail tomorrow, learn the next day, and the day after that – act."

(silence)

(man whispers)

"Genius!"

(shuts off the lights)

The next day

(ship's horn)

- Your Majesty, don't you think that we're making too much noise for your departure? The British are in Zanzibar, and they can probably hear you from there!
- Ah, Guten Morgen Karl, good to see you too! Did you sleep well?
- Your Majesty, I'm concerned about that the British would invade when you're away!
- So, what, I will return!

(both men pause)

- I have a plan. I want Britain to think I'm departing to go to Italy, we have already requested that they open up Gibraltar to us. Just so you know, Karl, I'm not boarding that ship.
- What? Then why are we here?
- To make noise, what if I don't board, but the British think that I'm away?
- They would invade and you would be here to stop them.
- Correct, I thought about that, and decided not to go with this plan, however. We will still lose if we do this, it's just going to take years.
- What's the plan now, sire?
- Well, Karl, I want you to rule temporarily, you have helped me out in all departments, so you will do a good job! Just don't declare mobilization, it would provoke the British.

(man nods head)

- Listen Karl, I will go on a separate ship, but the British don't know about that. I will go to Italian East Africa, and from there I will board one of their ships, which would allow us to pass through the Suez and reach Rome faster!

- Genius, your Majesty, you are a genius!
- I will pretend like I'm boarding, but I will really depart after an hour. After that, the Empire falls on your shoulders and what is on top of them!

Hours later

(Italian speaking)

(man approaches another man)

- Your Majesty, you're ready to board! Enjoy your journey to Rome!
- Grazie!

(two people enter a ship)

(man enters his cabin)

(man writes on paper)

"Somalia looks interesting, but I assume it would be very hard to defend. If Italy ends up at war with France and Britain, they will for sure lose their colonies in East Africa. Perhaps, the Italians are not the best allies, as when they're defeated, we would be all alone on the continent.

The Italian officers stationed in Somalia did let me know that Eritrea is pretty mountainous, so I assume Italy can defend it for a while. Still, our goal is to reclaim Germany, and the Italians are not in a favorable position to do that.

Austria is in the Italian sphere of influence…"

(chuckles)

"Oh God, how the tables have turned. Italy and Austria attacking Germany, going from Bavaria to Denmark is difficult, we need more allies. Czechoslovakia would be a great option, as they have the longest frontline with the Germans…"

(sips liquid out of glass)

"The thing is that the Czechoslovaks wouldn't have anything to gain out of this. The New Germany, under democracy, sounds to be doing even worse than the time we left. I need to ask the Duce about this situation.

I don't know if I want alliance, but what other option do we have, apart from the Soviet Union itself? Unless there is a change of leadership in France, we cannot work with them either. The Russians... Poland separates Germany and Russia, but the poles are unwilling to crave to one side, so they will sit as a buffer.

While I don't like how Italy would get defeated quickly in Africa, if all goes well, only allying with them would secure us the victory we're looking towards! Gott mit uns!"

Weeks later

(lighthouse horn)

(ship horn)

(Italian speaking)

- Your Majesty, we are in Napoli. A train is waiting for you and will escort you to Rome, where we will be waiting for your arrival!
- Grazie mille!
- I see you were taking notes while travelling with us, sire!
- A man must keep learning while they're alive! Thank you for your help, Antonio.
- My pleasure, your Majesty!

(man boards a train)

(man writes on paper)

"Napoli is truly a beautiful city! Everything that I heard about it is true, even one captain who said that the smell is the worst, he is right!

I have decided I want to secure an alliance with the Italians, as we can work together to achieve our goals! What are our goals? Well, I know mine, but I don't know the ones of Mussolini.

He did rise to power because Italy didn't receive enough land in the Great War. I would assume that he's looking to get back at France and Britain. Considering that, as a former Entente country, Italy still has good relations with them. No need to theorize and hurt my brain doing so, in a couple of hours, we will meet!

God, Italy is beautiful, but Germany is even more beautiful! Gott mi tuns!"

The next day

(trumpet)

(festival noise)

(Italian speaking)

(cheering)

"The Italians are such welcoming people" – thought to myself - "They seem to want me here! If all doesn't work out, at least there were many people who saw me in Rome, with pictures being taken. Britain now knows where I am, or most importantly, where I'm not. Should they strike their shot, I will be home in less than 2 weeks, they will really underestimate the situation! We will win!"

Hours later

- Your Majesty, the Duce of Fascism, Savior of the Italian People, Benito Mussolini, is ready to receive you!
- Bonjorno Signore Mussolini!

(both men pause for a second)

- You have no need for a translator it seems.

(both men laugh)

- I could use the help of one.

(both men shake hands)

- Nice to meet you, your Majesty! Here, have a seat.

(both men sit down)

- Your Majesty, I heard that you smoke cigars. I also know of your goal to return to mainland Germany. I have a special present for you! Open the drawer to your left!

(man opens drawer and pulls out a wooden box)

- Your Majesty, have you heard of Hermann Dietrich Upmann?
- No, I don't know him.
- In 1816, in Bielefeld, the world gave birth to this brilliant man. He reminds me of you! While I didn't know him personally, his ambition is inspiring, and his legacy lives on. Open the box.

(man opens box)

- Your Majesty, these cigars are H. Upmann, Hermann Upmann created this brand in Cuba. He was a banker and at 23 years of age he arrived in Cuba. After that he purchased a local cigar manufacturing factory in Havana, the capital city of Cuba, and started producing the product you're holding right now. The King of Spain, Don Alfonso XII, even praised him and gave him the title "Provider of His Majesty". Hermann Upmann couldn't stay in Cuba for so long, as he missed Germany, so after 4 years of staying in Cuba, he returned Bremen. This story remind me of you, your Majesty!

(both men pause)

- How come? He's just a German businessman.
- I would disagree, your Majesty. Cuba is further away from Germany than East Africa, I will tell you that much. Although that he found good life in

Cuba and could have stayed there, he wanted to return to his motherland, so do you! You can stay in East Africa, you have probably made it look like home, but you want to return? Why? Because Germany is your home!

(both men nod head)

(laugher)

(both men shake hands)

- I have no words, I understand now. This is really inspiring!
- Do you know what is also really inspiring, your majesty?
- What?
- That he returned successfully!

(silence)

(both men nod head)

- Your Majesty, I assume you didn't come here just to chat, so I suggest we get to the point of this. Do you want weapons from us, protection, alliance, or whatever?
- As you may know, the British are pushing fake news to their newspapers, justifying a war against the German Empire in Exile. I fear that they made invade. I have the manpower but lack the guns to equip these soldiers with. I was communicating with the Soviet Union regarding a possible purchase, but they won't arrive in time.
- Damn Communists, always late!
- Segnor Mussolini, if you have some spare weapons, I would like to purchase 50,000 rifles and get them as soon as possible. We can grab some on my way home, or even transfer some from Italian Somalia to the German Empire. Time of the essence.
- Did you come only to request guns? 50,000? You got it, you don't owe me anything! Flavio, come here!

(Italian speaking)

(door opens, door closes)

- These weapons will arrive in Der Es Salaam before your return.
- Wait, won't the British declare war on me once they find out?
- The British will not seize our cargo at the Suez Canal, as we can transport weapons to reach our colonies. Then once we drop them off at your Great Nation, Britain cannot intervene, as it's a simple trade between the 2 countries involved. Since they will arrive before you, they won't suspect it.
- This is smart! Appreciate the gesture, how can I pay you back if you're not interested in money?
- Your Majesty, I assume you have thought about the possibility of an alliance, correct?
- Yes, this is right!
- It takes a half-decent army General to know that it won't work out in the current terms. We have shared enemies, which is the former Entente, but if the Italians are go to war with them, Italian East Africa would be soon lost. Somalia is too flat to defend, and while some pockets may remain in Eritrea, you would be on your own. Correct me if I'm wrong.
- I agree here, Segnor Mussolini. I came to the same conclusion.
- Italy is not ready for war, neither are you. While you managed to rule over 10 million people, France and Britian, excluding their colonies, have many times more. Even if the Italians are involved, we still barely have a chance.

(man nods)

- Your Majesty, I don't know about you, but I think I have it figured out! Abyssinia is diving Italian East Africa in two. If we were to conquer it, we would have a big and unified African front against the enemy. Somalia and Eritrea alone would be hard to defend, but if we conquer Abyssinia together, we will resist.
- Because Abyssinia is mountainous, it may never fall if there is a possible war.
- Exactly!
- Your Majesty, we need to secure this operation together. This would benefit us and make talks of a future alliance possible, as we will be useful ally to you, and you will be one for us.

- I understand, it makes sense. Let us talk about it later, as now I have to deal with the British first. If there is an invasion of my Empire, I need to be there and defend it. Once the tread of Britain has subsided, we shall meet again and discuss how the German Empire can aid the Kingdom of Italy with their invasion of Abyssinia.
- That's more than what I wanted to hear! I'm looking towards a possible alliance, your Majesty!

(both men shake hands)

(door opens, door closes)

Meanwhile back in the German Empire in Exile

(man reads papers)

"Your Majesty, sir Wilhelm III, today, on the 18th of August 1923, the British have crossed into our territory from British East Africa. Reports from the frontlines say that Jasin, Kahe, and Kisangire are already lost. The is a battle ongoing for Amani and Tanga, with the British blockading and Der Es Salaam. They have taken advantage of your absence and are causing chaos.

I have taken your advice and ordered my soldiers not to fight in British East Africa. I have positioned them on the frontlines against British Northern Rhodesia and British Nyasaland. According to your prediction, we should be where the enemy doesn't expect us to be. We shouldn't fight on a front we're unprepared but catch them by surprise somewhere else! Most likely, their insertion into our land won't be too deep, as I predict they would run out of supplies.

The soldiers are ready and determined to liberate their homeland from the British. Many even want us to officially declare war and take land in the peace treaty, but I will hold out on this one, for now. Gott mit uns!"

(man flickers to the next page)

"Your Majesty, sir Wilhelm III, today, on the 26th of August 1923, we started our own invasion of British Northern Rhodesia and British Nyasaland. The enemy was caught by surprise, so the soldiers at Abercorn surrendered. We have reports that fighting has erupted in the capital of British Northern Rhodesia – Kasama. It looks favorable for our side. Regarding the northern front. I sent I small taskforce to British Uganda, with the coal to capture Buganda province. This is a worthy distraction, as on the front with British East Africa, action has stopped, as you have predicted. I have ordered my troops to take back the lost cities of Kahe, Kisangire, and Jasin. Gott mit uns!"

(man stops reading)

(man flickers to the next page)

"Your Majesty, sir Wilhelm III, today, on the 6th of September 1923, we managed to push into British East Africa, and occupied the city of Voi. This has cut the Ugandan railway in half. Now supplies cannot flow from Mombasa, the largest port in the area, to the capital Nairobi, and even further into Uganda and Lake Victoria. If we are to hold this position, soon, we will be victorious.

Right now, our side has 47,270 soldiers mobilized, most are well equipped, and all are determined to fight and defend their freedom. 82% of the army is native people, who hold hate against the British, just like we do.

We were pushed out of British Northern Rhodesia, due to a lack of a declaration of a war declaration by the enemy side. This looks like a border conflict, not an actual war. As a result, I have still ordered my troops to not completely fall back, so they're occupying Avercorn right now. Gott mit uns!"

(silence)

(man flickers to the next page)

"Your Majesty, sir Wilhelm III, today, on the 11th of September 1923, the British have announced that they want talks to end the border war and seize the conflict. This would mean that we would need to return to our positions, but we already occupied important towns in the continent. Due to your absence, I have made the executive decision to not take any land, except the city of Abercorn in British Northern Rhodesia.

The reason for that is even if we take Voi, which would really screw with the British supply in East Africa, once they have built a new railway, they will declare war and take revenge. Taking Zanzibar would be nice, but the British would never leave these islands. They give them an advantageous position of overlooking our most populous city, Der Es Salaam.

I may have secured just a tiny town in British Northern Rhodesia, but at least I hope that with that, the British won't have more justifications to invade us, at least for the time being! Soon we shall return to our motherland! Today, God saved the German Empire in Exile!"

Austrian rules Germany? This is fine!

"The Allied and Associated Governments affirm, and Germany accepts the responsibility for causing all the loss and damage as a consequence of the war imposed upon them by the aggression of Germany and her allies."

(man pauses)

- Germany didn't start this war and having to pay war reparations and losing 13% of their territory is unacceptable!

(man slams the table)

- I know, and I'm telling you, the Weimar Republic is the greatest failure brought upon the Germans! I know that I'm telling you, I know. I may be sitting in front of the mirror, talking to myself, but I know that all Germans are struggling because of this dysfunctional new state!

(man stops talking, so he could catch his breath)

- I know that the Weimar Republic has failed! How? Because I'm making millions of real money talking about these problems! The people are buying my book and are supporting my ideas! Yet I'm sitting in my home, talking to myself! I'm one of the greatest people ever born in this world! I should stive to unite the German speakers and save the Germans from their fate! With donations from wealthy Germans, the Nazi party is bigger and better! Everybody fears the communists! I swear, the Soviet Union must be more dysfunctional than the Weimar Republic, both states should not exist, and be replaced with the superior Aryan race, united under one banner!

(man puts on his jacket)

(door opens, door closes)

- Good morning Herr Hitler, can I help you with something?
- Nein, Frau Müller, Danke.

(man rushes down the stairs)

"1929, the Germans are going to remember this year! We were just starting to recover and now, because of irresponsible American lending, we're yet again impoverished. Germany isn't an independent country, we pay money to other countries and take loans from other countries, to do what with them? Pay other countries! The industry? It's mostly Germany, but not fully, same with the resources! God damn it, even the German territory isn't fully German. These damn Frenchmen occupy the Saarland and take our precious coal and steel resources for their own benefit, while the German people struggle!

What in Germany is truly German is the people and the language! We need a strong and united Germany, under one strong Aryan leader, not this democratic dysfunctional system."

(man stops and sits at a bench in a park)

(silence)

(a woman walking a dog passes by)

(man jumps out of his seat and pets the dog)

- What breed is he? – asked the man.
- He doesn't have a bread, he is mixed.
- Huh? Why don't you get a German Sheppard, the purest and most German bread in the whole world!

(silence)

(woman walks away, appearing rushed)

"God damn it, nothing in this nation is pure! Even the politics, oh the politics of Germany! We have a president that under Article 48 does reforms in desperate attempt to save the country, but nothing, and I mean nothing seems to work out!

The Nazi party is growing stronger and stronger! We're among the most pure, honest, and forward-looking individuals in all of Germany, and only we, can save the country!"

Years later

Back in the German Empire in Exile

(man reads newspaper)

"On 30 January 1933, Reich President Paul von Hindenburg appoints Adolf Hitler as Reichskanzler. The new Reichskanzler Hitler addresses the German nation in a call of the Reichsregierung, broadcast over all German transmitters on 2 days later."

"At the risk of appearing to talk nonsense I tell you that the National Socialist movement will go on for 1,000 years! ... Don't forget how people laughed at me 15 years ago when I declared that one day I would govern Germany. They laugh now, just as foolishly, when I declare that I shall remain in power!"

"Berlin is on fire! On the 27th of February 1933, at exactly 9pm. both the Reichstag and the Imperial Palace were set on fire! The German chancellor Adolf Hitler claims that this event was staged by the communist opposition, who are planning a violent uprising. Emergency legislation is needed to prevent this from happening!"

(man looks up from the newspaper)

(man shouted)

- These animals! How could they burn the Imperial Palace!

(man bangs on table)

"Hitler and the Nazi party will take over Germany. Paul Von Hindenburg is old and they manipulate him. They forced him to enact policies regarding abandoning trade unions, freedom of protests, banning all political parties, and everything. To me, this is clear, they're establishing a dictatorship."

(man lights a cigar)

- H. Upmann, thank you Mussolini.

"This isn't the communist revolution I wished for, but this new German state looks to be really tyrannical. I really hope that soon France and Britian would bash heads with this new Germany, so that I can intervene and secure a place in my beloved homeland!"

(man stands up)

(door opens, door closes)

(knocks on door)

- Ja.
- Guten Abend, Karl.
- Hello, your Majesty, what brings you here?
- I need you to mobilize 50,000 soldiers and arrange a meeting with the Italian Duce, I want to arrive as soon as possible.
- On it, sire. Will do my best for you to depart tomorrow morning!
- Danke, Karl, Gute Nacht!
- Gute Nacht!

(door opens, door closes)

"I need to act quickly…"

(man sits in chair)

(lights a cigar)

"If I don't act quickly, this new Hitler guy and Benito Mussolini might want to do something together, although I doubt it. Hitler has claimed that he wants to unite all the German speakers under one country, which would be his version of Germany.

Meanwhile, the Italians hold South Tyrol, predominantly inhabited by German-speakers. Austria is also an Italian protectorate, or sort of. Germany cannot go far with an alliance with Italy if my assumptions are right.

We should enact our plan to invade and annex Abyssinia, so that Italy is in a stronger position in Africa, which would hopefully secure their position in the region."

Abyssinia or Ethiopia? Neither!

A month later, in Rome

- Your Majesty, it's good to have you back! I wanted to personally congratulate you on your efforts of defending yourself and your Glorious Nation against the British invades years ago! Here, have a seat, do you want something? Wine, something to smoke, women?

(laugher)

- I don't need anything, but I want to talk to you about something.
- What, do you want to marry me?

(laugher)

- Signore Mussolini, I wanted to ask you about your opinion regarding the events of the new Germany.
- Oh, this Hitler guy? He's a clown! Just a public figure, doesn't know what he is talking about. Or he does know but knows he cannot achieve this. Without counting, I can bet that over 10 other sovereign countries have a solid Germany minority, what is he going to do, invade them all?

(laugher)

- Isn't the Kingdom of Italy one of them, considering South Tyrol?
- Hey!

(silence)

- South Tyrol is Italian, but there are many German-speakers living there!
- Yes, exactly what I wanted to say!
- Austria too, this Hitler guy I assume would soon want Austria to join Germany. Considering the political situation in the country, he may succeed. I swear half the parties in there are for pro-unification. The Christian Social Party, headed by Anton Rintelen had a bit over than 30% of the vote if I remember correctly. Hitler is not a friend, but my number

one danger right now, and I assume the same would apply to you too, am I right, your Majesty?

(silence)

(man nods head)

- Signore Mussolini, I came here to tell you that I also thought about this and I predicted how you would react to this New Germany. This is why I can suggest that we move forward with our plan to subjugate Abyssinia. I have told my commanders to prepare 50,000 troops. With your permission, they can be transferred to Somalia, where they would be ready to fight on your side.
- Great news, I love to hear that, your Majesty! By the way, your Italian has improved, you should visit more often.

(man nods head)

- Your Majesty, with your help, we can declare war once you get back, or even sooner if you'd like. I prefer to attack in the winter, the conditions aren't too brutal, unlike the summer. I have heard of soldiers dying on their duty just because of how hot it gets.
- Back home, we suffer from the same problems. Our troops are comprised mostly of natives which means that they're used to these conditions. We shouldn't wait around, but get to acting as soon as possible!
- We will schedule an invasion for late 1934, so our troops can also participate, your Majesty. If we invade in the summer, it will be only you who will be fighting.

(both men nod head)

(both men shake hands)

(door opens, door closes)

Days later

(man writes on paper)

"I think I managed to secure an alliance with Italy, or an arrangement that works for both of us for the time being. I'm glad that him and Hitler have many disagreements, this would make it impossible for them to unite. Out of the two, Italy does look like the stronger nation, they have their politics figured out. This new Germany is chaotic and tyrannical. I heard they're not focusing on improving the lives of the people but are rather investing in their army.

Hitler doesn't want to produce any domestic industry. It looks more likely that he would conquer other sovereign nations instead. Mussolini has assured me that if Austria is one of these nations, he will resist. I promised him that we would intervene on his side and declare war on this Tyrannical Germany. Gott mit uns!"

1 month later

(man reads newspaper)

"An European power at war. This time, it's not Germany who is the aggressive power in Europe, but the Italians. The last time an European country was at war were the Soviets, who were fighting their civil war, and the Turks, who were fighting their war of independence against Greece. All of this was officially finished in 1923.

Now, almost 11 years later, the Italians have invaded a neutral country in Africa, the state of Abyssinia. Let us not forget that in the Berlin Conference of 1885, Italy as awarded perhaps more of Africa than what they deserved, now they're looking to expand their influence and connect their colonies of Italian Eritrea and Italian Somalia.

The British and the French governments have pledged to suspend their alliance treaties with the Kingdom of Italy, and renew them only once Abyssinia, now called Ethiopia, is a free nation again!"

- Huh.

(silence)

1 months later

(man reads newspaper)

"Dutch Marines preparing to leave Rotterdam for the Saar. The League of Nations Council determined that a peacekeeping force would be necessary for the plebiscite period. The Saarland was occupied by France after the end of the Great War, and now, with the new German Chancellor, people want to return to their motherland!

On the 13th of January 1935, the people of the Saarland would vote on the future of the territory. They can choose between uniting with Germany, maintaining the status-que, or joining France. Only time will tell what the German public in the Saarland would decide."

(man puts down newspaper)

(door opens, door closes)

(man walks down the stairs)

(man sits on a bench, in a park)

"The weather is nice today. You will always hear me complain about this, how have I not become used to it already, I don't know. Germany... ahhh the German nation, what are they doing now? The French are obviously not going to let them have the Saarland. I know that many German communist opposition parties reside there, so they can escape the tyranny of the German Reich, or the New Germany.

Hitler is a smart man it appears, he will try to secure this territory, as it would allow for him to completely eliminate the political opposition in my country. Bastard! Are there any German monarchists even present in Germany right now? I need to see Karl."

(man goes up the stairs)

(man knocks on door)

(silence)

(man knocks on door again)

"Where is he?"

(man knocks on door again)

(silence)

"Will check back later."

(a man rushes out of nowhere)

- Hey, your Majesty, were you looking for me?
- I was, what's going on?
- Just got off the phone with the soldiers in the Abyssinian front, it's not looking too good. Our army is performing brilliantly in the south, but the Italians are more or less struggling in the north. I would suggest that we divert our forces from one front to the other, so that we can take Abyssinia evenly. Right now our troops are occupying useless desert, and our allies are fighting in the mountains. Do we support them?
- What do the Italian officers suggest?
- They say we should advance to Addis Ababa and take it, but it can result in thousands of casualties.
- Do it.

(man nods head)

- Wait, you needed to talk to me, correct, sire?
- Indeed, Karl, let's go inside.
- You have read the news of the German attempt to take back the Saarland, right?
- Right?
- Well, I don't think that France is simply going to give it to them, it produces a lot of resources for the French and adds free manpower to their pool. This is very important for the French, right?
- Right, your Majesty.

- It's also important for Hitler, as in the Saarland you have his political opponents and other political parties, that are banned in Germany, hiding.

(man nods head)

- Karl, I'm trying to say that the Saarland is very important for both sides, so it can become a hotspot. Another World War can erupt from that, which can become our opportunity.
- Your Majesty, don't you think that if that were to happen, Germany would get crushed easily? After all the German Imperial Army is not present, and the Germans are limited to 100,000 soldiers by Versailles. The French can easily conquer them alone, so they won't need our help. Your Majesty, I would suggest that you make a public appearing before the election and urge people to want for unification. Hitler doesn't like the monarchy, because he thinks that we surrendered too early, but he has respect for us. We can use that.
- How exactly?
- Hitler will most likely not censor your message, especially if it aligns with his goal. You should say that the Germans vote to join the Saar and to Germany. This would delay a possible war between France and Germany, which would work to your benefit?
- And how does a stronger Germany benefit me?
- A stronger Germany would even the scales in terms of a war between them and France, and once you join the French side, you will tip the scales. You should play both sides and make sure they remain even in terms of strength, while you ensure you grow stronger. This makes sense!

(both men nod head)

- Hey Karl, make sure to figure out how to win in Ethiopia, I will take care of this personally.
- Understood, your Majesty!

Days later

(man reads newspaper)

"Following the referendum, the Council of the League of Nations decided that the Saar should return to Germany no later than the 1st of March, 1935. 90.73% voted for unification with Germany, with 8.86% wanting to maintain the status quo, and at last, 0,4% voted for a unification with France. Josef Bürckel would become Reichskommissarof the territory. What a wonderful day to be a German!"

- Huh? What a wonderful day to be a German, you say?
- Your Majesty, I heard that France is pretty pissed about the situation, and the communist opposition in France is growing and getting stronger. It's entirely in the realm of the possibilities that France goes communist, perhaps they would ally with the Soviet Union. We remain allied with Italy, with the United Kingdom also being able to support our cause. They're more anti-communist than anti-Germany or anti-Kaiser.
- Good. What a shame about the Saarland. I remember I forced my father to suggest to France that they occupy it, so that the New Germans pays less in reparations. Hitler is slowly undoing the harm of the Versailles treaty, which we created only to weaken the New Germany. Each day it becomes more and more difficult for us to catch up to the Nazis in Europe.

(pause)

- So, Karl, what's the matter in Ethiopia?
- Great news actually. We have suffered around 1000 casualties in the 4 months of fighting, with the enemy side suffering at least 10 times more, excluding civilians. Haile Selassie and his family have left the country. They will either seek international support, or just hide. Even if they seek international support, nobody will come to their aid. France is on the verge of a communist takeover, Britain is too shaken up, Germany has its own problems, and the Soviets are just plain incompetent. 3 days after that, Marshal Pietro Badoglio led Italian troops into Addis Ababa. Mussolini had declared an Italian victory and Ethiopia to be an Italian province.
- Good, the war is almost over.

- Officially, it looks like it. There's still going to be a lot of rebels, but the Italians would have to deal with that, unless they request our support.
- Great news! Now we and the Italians have the strongest presence in the continent, so far, we're unchallenged! The German Empire in Exile shall return, sooner or later!

In dire need of a Naval Admiral...

(man reads newspaper)

"On the 7th of March, the German army was ordered to cross into the Rhineland, which was supposed to be a demobilized zone. This is a clear violation of the treaty of Versailles. Hitler is out of control! I would predict that he would go for France and Poland next, as he would be looking to reclaim his lost lands! This man is the greatest threat to the stability and prosperity of the continent of Europe, not the Soviet Union. I pray for peace!"

(silence)

- The New Germany's back at it again?
- Seems like it...
- Listen, let's go out for a walk.

(door opens, door closes)

(goes down the stairs)

- I should meet with Mussolini and perhaps stay there. We need to formalize our alliance, so Germany knows not to expand into our direction.
- For how long do you expect to be gone, your Majesty?
- I don't know, but I'm sure you will do an amazing job governing the Empire. Since we're here, the population has almost doubled, which is a great accomplishment. 15 million people now call the German Empire in Exile home, with 92% being natives. The economy is at the strongest it's ever been. With this Hitler guy being just 3 years in charge, he has done plenty to destabilize the continent of Europe.
- If everything that he says in his book is true, the whole continent of Europe would lose its light and fall to darkness for the time to come.
- Did you hear that he claimed that the National Socialist regime would last a thousand years?
- No, I haven't.

- We need to change that! While I'm alive I will not allow for this!
- When are you leaving for the Kingdom of Italy, your Majesty?
- You know the drill, Karl, I'm going tomorrow morning.
- Will have everything ready.
- I can always rely on you!
- Always

(both men sit at a bench in a park)

- Karl, what do you think is Hitler's next move?
- I think he would go after Luxembourg or Austria, with Luxembourg maybe being the most likely option.
- Why is that?
- He has claimed that he wants to unify all the German speaking countries, both Luxembourg and Austria are predominantly German speaking, unlike regions from France, Switzerland, Poland, and Czechoslovakia. There is no other option for him right now. If he does neither of what I just said, he's a hypocrite!
- Good thinking, I will present this logic to Mussolini, as he would want to hear it. I would aim to create an alliance with the Italians. We should include Austria and if we can Hungary too. The Hungarians lost a lot of land after the war, so I assume due to irridentist claims, they cannot ally with any of their bordering countries. Unless they want to be defeated again, they will join us.
- Your Majesty, your trips to the Kingdom of Italy have increased in quantity lately. It takes you between two and three weeks to get there on one way, and then the same time to go back. We have money to purchase a plane, which will take you from here to Rome in half the time, would you like to?
- No, Karl, this is unreliable transport. For me to take so long to get to Rome is good, not bad, as you claim it is. I think that this is my unfair advantage, it takes me a long time to reach Europe, so when I'm there, I do what I set out to. I also go only when needed, not when I can. There is no urgency right now, it can wait.

Weeks later, in Rome

- How come that Italy and Rome is more and more beautiful every time I visit, Signor Mussolini?
- Ideology! The Italian fascists are clean people, unlike the tyrannical German fascists! They're killing off the opposition, the minorities they don't like and all that. I heard that when Hitler rose to power, one of the first things that he did is he increased the wage of all Germans by 10.9%, but to compensate for that in the budget, he raided Jewish homes, stealing their jewelry, precious artwork, and everything they deemed valuable. This is how the Nazi German economy runs, not by producing, but by stealing!
- This means we should take action.
- What do you mean, your Majesty?
- Sooner or later, Hitler will run our of people to steal from within his own country. If this is the way he truly operates, as a logical next step, he would try to takeover independent countries.

(both men nod)

- And he would enslave their people too, steal their national reserve and all that...
- Signor Mussolini, I think that the logical next step for him is to either invade Luxembourg or Austria. Both are predominantly German, and considering his goal of uniting the German speakers, all checks out for a possible invasion.
- This can explain why he's so interested in militarizing heavily...

(both men nod)

- Even if Luxembourg is first to be attacked, it would only delay the Nazi invasion of Austria. Luxembourg doesn't have a lot of wealth and population, so after a couple of months, the Nazis would run out of money again. Austria would be next. Speaking of that, how's the situation there?
- We're almost fully in charge. The government's ideology is similar to ours and they resist Nazi pressure at annexation. The Nazis did try to coup Austria 2 years ago, but they failed miserably. I don't know if you've

heard, but I put an end to that. I personally stopped the whole regime from taking Austria!
- Yes, I read that, congratulations!
- Gracie!

(silence)

- Signor Mussolini, I came here to request for us to form an official alliance. We should strive to include Austria and maybe even Hungary. We should stand as a one single and united block against the Nazi aggression.

(silence)

- Good.

(pause)

- Your Majesty, I was thinking of exactly the same thing! I already tasked by bureaucrats with writing protocols in Rome for said alliance. Austria and Hungary said that they're interested, so it's up to us to do the initial work and prove our worth!
- When are the protocols going to be ready?
- You want to take them back home, I understand. Let me go and ask. Mario, can you deal with that!
- Si, Signore.

(door opens, door closes)

- What is the premise of the protocols?
- We can just refer to them as the Rome Protocols, for now. The premise is as you said, to stop Nazi expansion, together we shall stand united. I also included a clause in for the dismantling of the Kingdom of Yugoslavia. The Kingdom of Italy, the Federal State of Austria, and the Kingdom of Hungary all claim lands from Yugoslavia. So, we wish to dismember it among ourselves. Hope you don't have anything against that.

(man nods)

- Doesn't it make sense to also reach out to Bulgaria for that goal too?
- Tsar Boris is too stubborn to involve his country into an alliance of any kind. This I think would be the biggest downfall of his nation. All countries around his Kingdom are in some sort of an alliance with each other, he's too isolated, but yet he doesn't take action. This guy married Giovanna of Savoy, the literal daughter of King Victor Emanuel III in 1930. I personally attended their wedding. This should have secured an alliance with the Bulgarians, but to no avail.
- Do you think that I can somehow help with that? Boris is part of the House of Saxe-Coburg and Gotha, fellow Germans.
- Unless you kill him and his father takes over, nothing can be done, for now.

(knocks on door)

- Si!
- Signor Mussolini, the documents are ready.

(places a couple of paper sheets on the table)

- Excellent work, now go rest! Here you can read through it!

(man hands paper to his friend)

"Protocol No. 1: the signatories must confer together on all problems which particularly concern them, and on problems of a general character. A friendship treaty must be signed with all participating nations, where each one would agree and recognize the existence of the other nations' claims to territory and sphere of influence. As to prevent a Nazi takeover, or any other tread, each participating country has the rights to hold joint consultations whenever at least one of them deems it desirable.

Protocol No. 2: Don't place any economic restrictions on participating countries. Assist the Hungarian government, because of falling wheat prices. To facilitate the rapid transit of goods in the Adriatic Sea. Establish a commission of experts, who would jointly propose economic policies."

(man puts papers down)

- So, your Majesty, do you think that this can serve your people?
- I think it would, we can benefit from that. Right now, we don't have any trading partners and we're self-sufficient. While this is good news to hear, our economy has hit a cap, so, we cannot grow further. We can purchase Hungarian wheat and sell it across Africa, which would hopefully improve the situation for all parties involved.
- Do you want to sign it right now?
- Yes, let us stay strong against the Nazis and their influence!

(pen signs paper)

(both men shake hands)

(door opens, door closes)

Back in the German Empire in Exile

- Karl, I think we're doing just fine.
- I agree, your Majesty. Ever since we're here, the quality of life has improved, and the natives are praising us. We're not seen by them as gods, but as equals, and we don't view them as slaves. They all wish us luck to return to our homeland and genuinely support us.

(throws rock into the lake)

- I returned from Rome, we will work together with Mussolini to defend Austria. Regarding Luxembourg, it's in the French backyard, so if something were to happen there, they will deal with it.
- All is looking in our favor so far!
- Good. Speak to you tomorrow, Karl.
- Gute Nacht, your Majesty!

The next day

(knocks on door)

(silence)

- Oh there you are!
- Your Majesty, I think we've found Hitler's next move. Read this!

(man hands another man a newspaper)

"Spain is on fire!"

(flickers to the next page)

"After the Popular Front narrowly won the Spanish Election of 1936, the revolutionary left-wing masses took to the streets and freed prisoners. So far, 16 people have been killed by police officers, who are trying to maintain order.

The opposition of the Popular Front views Spain as a socialist Republic, which should ally with the Soviet Union. With such opposing views, as well as the present issue with the Basque and Catalan nationalities, Spain is in an open revolt. If they had to be described with one word, it would be – anarchy!"

- Hah? You think that Hitler did that? The Spanish have always been incompetent people, no matter if it's a Republic or a Monarchy. This is between themselves, Hitler is not involved.
- Hitler may not have caused it, but he can intervene.
- Why do you think that, Karl?
- Well, your majesty, fascism seems to be on the rise in Europe, look at the Kingdom of Italy, the Federal States of Austria, and of course, Home...

(silence)

- Your Majesty, Spain looks like it can have a Fascist takeover and you can bet that Hitler would make sure that these Fascists are allied to him, instead of to Italy.

(silence)

- I think it's too hard to predict, but I do agree it's not looking good so far. Keep me updated on the situation, I want to know what's going on!
- Will do, sire!

2 weeks later

- Your Majesty, do you remember the situation in Spain?
- I do actually, anything new you have to report?
- Nothing concrete, just a theory. Army generals in Spain, among which is Emilio Mola are planning a counter coup. The Republican government is planning to give more autonomy to the minorities, which is seen by the Spanish Falanga as a tread to Spain's existence, hence why they want to coup the government.
- So, if they were to succeed, Spain will become a military dictatorship, correct?
- It looks like it.
- Then it's only a problem for Portugal I guess, not for us. Not every conflict that occurs in the world concerns us. The Japanese and Chinese are fighting, but I don't hear reports from there, this is maybe because it doesn't concern our situation. We need to choose what we want to worry about, and for now, Spain is none of our business.
- Your Majesty, I think that context is important, and it matters. The Nazis used to support the Republic of China, so we can assume that if a big war were to break out, perhaps the Chinese would join the Nazis.
- You're too optimistic, and even if they do, I don't think they will do too much.

(another report from Spain arrives in the following days)

"The Popular Front saw what was happening and decided to take measures into their own hands. Emilio Mola was moved from head of the Army of Africa to military governor in a city in the Navarre province. Francisco Franco stopped being the Chief of Staff and was transferred command of the Canary Islands.

The Popular Front and the Falanga started assassinating each other's political figures. With many dead, the unrest in Spain is far from being over."

(another report from Spain arrives 2 weeks later)

"José Calvo Sotelo was the leader of the monarchist party, and he was brutally murdered. Allegedly the police were involved in the murder. People suspect that the Popular Front is getting rid of their enemies.

This looks to have provoked some army generals, among which is the respectable Francisco Franco and Emilio Mola. Spanish Morocco looks to be in an open revolt against the Republican government. Only time will tell us if both sides would meet to negotiate their differences!"

5 days later

- Kaiser, come and read this out loud, I don't believe what I'm seeing!
- The Nationalists, led by Francisco Franco already control nearly 1/3 of the country.

(silence)

- Well, Karl, I still don't see the big deal. Let me look at the map.

(man hands a map to other man)

- So, the rebels, or the Nationalists as they call themselves control the colonies and the Eastern part of Spain, which is among the poorest. They don't control Madrid, nor Barcelona. I think that they're screwed.
- You think so?
- Looking at it, the Republican government still controls the arms industry and should have the manpower advantage.
- Do you think that Hitler would intervene?
- I think it's unlikely. We knew months in advance that there was going to be a civil war in Spain, but we didn't know how it would play out. This is why the Europeans signed the Non-Intervention Agreement. The Nazis also signed it. Ships that arrive to Spain would be checked if they contain any weapons. It should become impossible for them to smuggle arms and support the Nationalists.
- What about the Italians?

- What about them?
- Won't they support the Nationalists, considering that they are nationalists themselves?

(silence)

- Go and ask Mussolini what his intent is, and to win us a favor, tell him that we will support him in whatever decision he comes up with.
- Understood, your Majesty.

Days later

"Report on the situation in Spain.

The Italians have said that they want to intervene and secure an ally in Iberia. They want to work with the Nationalists and have already started smuggling weapons into the Iberian Peninsula."

Days later

"Report on the situation in Spain.

The Nazis have appeared out of nowhere and are also supporting Nationalist Spain. They are the country that managed to smuggle the most into the Iberian Peninsula. This move could start a world war if the Nazis continue to play with their luck. The Germans are not only sending soldiers, but training Spanish Nationalists, and also sending equipment.

We must seize our support of the Nationalists, as if we want to beat Nazis and gain the support of the Nationalists, we will need to help them more than the Nazis. This is frankly impossible to happen, as it would provoke international outrage. France and Britain may start seeing us as the bad guys, instead of the Nazis.

This is why I suggest we support the Carlist wing within Spain. The other alternative is to support the Republic and demand for representatives with positions of power, but it won't work out. This is because the Soviets can contribute more power and influence to the Republicans.

We cannot dominate any of the two fighting sides, so we should support an entirely different faction. The Carlists are monarchists, who would want to work with the German Empire in Exile, and in fact, can be a great asset.

The other option is reserved only in case the Carlists don't want to work it us, and it's that if we cannot have Spain, we should make it weaker. This is why if all goes bad, we should support the Catalan and Basque independence movements, which should make Nazi Germany or the Soviet Union control less of Spain."

3 weeks later

"The Spanish Carlists have risen up and are in an open conflict against the Republican Government, but also against the Nationalist Falanga.

This really complicated the situation for the Nationalists, as they lost a huge chunk of their northern territory. Right now the major cities of Santander, Bilbao, Vitoria, and Pamplona are under Carlist rule. There is a Carlist offensive ongoing against the Nationalists, who control the city of Valladolid.

Both sides are fighting desperately for it, as controlling this city would allow for a more effective incursion into the enemy's territory.

If the Nationalists lose this city, they can be cut in half, with the province of Galicia being separated from the mainland."

5 days later

"The Spanish Nationalists, the Heroes of the Iberian Peninsula, have not only successfully defended Valladolid against the Carlist invaders, but have managed to do an effective counterattack, where the port city of Bilbao was taken. This leaves the city of Pamplona to be encircled.

As the encircled divisions were fighting desperately, losing battle after battle, they were cornered next to the French border, where they escaped successfully. This would for sure create a diplomatic incident, with all of Western Europe disagreeing on the matter."

The next day

"The Condor Legion are a Nazi supported group, fighting alongside Nationalist Spain. They were useful in the Battle of Toledo, but there is no denying that these people are warmongers. We have evidence that the Bombing of Guernica was initiated by Nazi Germany.

This bombing will go down in history as the deadliest one so far. Large part of the town has been destroyed, and more than a thousand people have immediately died as a result of that."

2 days after that

"The Carlist soldiers that had fled to France have declared an independent country for the Basque people, requesting that all Basque nationalists rise. This is partially in response to the bombings on Guernica, but also because they can go hiding into France when they want.

While the Spanish Nationalists and the Nazi Germans are not content with this, they cannot do anything about it right now. The French helping out the Basque rebels has resulted in a lot of turmoil back home. The French have among the highest communist oppositions in the world, any wrong move and France may flip to the other side.

Since the Socialist world is predominantly supporting the Republican Spanish in this conflict, they view France's action of housing rebels as a threat. A civil war in France can follow if the situation continues to escalate!"

24 hours later

"The Basque have reclaimed Navarre province, but the Nationalists have just taken Madrid. Republican Spain is being dismantled as we're speaking. The Independent State of Catalunya has also risen, who demand peace in the Iberian Peninsula.

The Catalan people are ready to defend themselves against the Spanish Republic and the Spanish Nationalists, but do not seek conflict, they want to reclaim the borders of the Catalunya state. They have claimed that they will not push any further.

2 weeks later

"Barcelona has officially fallen to the Independent State of Catalunya. The Republican Government is left only with the major city of Valencia. Against all odds, the Nationalists have arisen and managed to come out on top. This was at the cost of Spain losing the Basque and Catalan nationalities, who have declared their own state.

Considering the ideology of the Spanish Nationalist, sooner or later, they will start reclaiming these new states."

Crisis, crisis, crisis!

(man reads a report, sent directly from Rome)

(man lights cigar)

"The Rome protocols would get expanded into Bulgaria and Albania as of the beginning of 1938. This move wouldn't be without its fair share of controversy. It would see the revival of the Little Entente, which was originally an alliance against the Hungarians, during their communist period. The Balkan Pact, which was an alliance against Bulgaria, may also see it's revival. Our enemies in the region would be Czechoslovakia, Romania, Yugoslavia, and Greece.

While this may sound concerning, let us not forget that the main enemy is Nazi Germany. If we were to fight the Little Entente alone, we would have the upper hand. If we were to fight Nazi Germany alone, we would have the upper hand. It's only concerning if we end up fighting both Nazi Germany and the Little Entente, which should be impossible.

Hitler would claim parts of Czechoslovakia, which should prevent a possible alliance in the future. For now, we shouldn't fear the German incursion into Austria."

(man pours liquid into glass)

(man writes a response on a piece of paper)

"I have signed the Rome protocols. All participating nations are now allied against the Nazi tread, so we should be secure. This could be further from the truth. Hitler will not take Luxembourg, as he has set his sights to Austria. We should call an emergency situation, and each member of the Rome Protocols should contribute some amount of their army to defend Austria, in case a possible invasion occurs in the near future."

A couple of days later

(man reads a report)

"We have discussed the situation and Austria will commit to building fortifications on the German border, while neglecting other parts of their economy. We will support the Austrian economy with cheap resources from the German Empire in Exile, manpower from the Kingdom of Italy, and cheap grain from the Tsardom of Bulgaria and the Kingdom of Hungary."

(man pours liquid into glass)

(door opens, door closes)

(goes down the staircase)

(peace)

(silence)

(man sits next to a man on a bench)

- Hello Karl, what are you doing here this late into the night?
- About the same as you, I assume. I feel uneasy and I cannot go to sleep, so I decided to come here and watch the ducks in the lake.
- What are you on about, we're growing stronger, we have allies and influence, why worry?
- But what if we don't?
- It doesn't matter because we do have it!

(silence)

- Your Majesty, I don't think that Hitler would give up just because of the Rome Protocols. He is a madman and I'm sure that he would at least try and go down with the ship if he has to. Nazi Germany will invade Austria soon! They have been justifying this for years to their public.
- What... why are you saying this? We have fortified Austria, it's about impossible to take. Listen Karl, France built the Maginot wall, which should help them against in a possible war with Nazi Germany. These bastards, they want to defend themselves and not go on the offense! We have replicated that in Austria, but we have the terrain advantage. Even

if Germany were to invade, they wouldn't get far! I will go as far as to say that they would do us a favor if they invade, I wish that could happen!
- But what if the Nazis don't invade?
- Why wouldn't they?
- Because they don't have to.

(silence)

- Your Majesty, 4 years ago, in 1934, the Germans tried to coup Austria. While Benito Mussolini stepped up and secured the Austrian independence, Engelbert Dollfuss, the Chancellor of Austria, was assassinated in the coup.
- Right.
- Well, now you have Kurt Schuschnigg as the Chancellor of Austria, but there is a problem. Do you know where he was born?
- I do not, no. I actually never met him, we just communicate via telegraph.
- He was born in Riva del Garda, do you know where this is?
- I have no idea.
- It's in Italy, the Trentino province – South Tyrol.
- Hmmmm...

(silence)

- So, you question his loyalty?
- I'm just bringing it up, as I doubt that even Mussolini knows that, unless he has asked somebody to figure it out. If I were in his shoes, I would demand that my country includes within its borders my birth city. Look, all I'm saying is if anyone has irredentist claims, it's definitely Austria, considering their dictator's place of birth.
- I need to speak with Mussolini about that. I think that Kurt Schuschnigg is a reasonable man. It's unlikely that he would abandon us to join Nazi Germany. If he does it, South Tyrol can become occupied by the Germans for the time being, but Austria wouldn't exist. I have heard that he's an Australian nationalist.
- Your Majesty, all I'm saying is that you may have the best fortifications on the border, but Vienna is vulnerable to fall to a coup. The number of

Austrians who get radicalized and have favorable views of Nazi Germany is increasing, a coup against the government is the biggest weakness of the alliance, and I don't see how we can prevent that from happening.

(silence)

- I will think about it, Karl.
- Good night, your Majesty, and don't stay up too late.

(door opens, door closes)

"Ah, the giraffe, been a while since I saw one. This reminds me that I need to go on hunting trips more frequently, but not to kill giraffes of course. I thought I discovered my unfair advantage, but now I don't even remember what it was. I have either lost it, or never had it in the first place then.

Well, what is the enemy's unfair advantage? They have millions of radicalized people, ready to die for the Führer any minute. The former Entente seems to have a more favorable view of him, rather than of me. They haven't fought him, yet, then they will come looking for me!

A traitor in Austria, how can I prevent that? The Austrians are clearly a weakened state after the war, so they sought after to join a stronger German state, where they will be equal partners. What if I do that too? What if I become the ruler of Austria. No, this is too risky. I'm right next to the Nazis. But I do have my allies…"

(pulls out a wooden box from the drawer)

"The last one…"

(lights cigar with matches)

(exhales)

"I should at least visit Austria, to make sure that I secure a lot of support there. This can allow for a monarchist party to form and with a lot of luck, we can oust Kurt Schuschnigg and his irredentist claims! No. That's too risky. Austria is filled with Nazi and pro-unification sympathizers. I'm asking to get assassinated. Hm, but if I am assassinated, would this lead to another war? Does this benefit the German Empire in Exile?"

(pours liquid into glass)

"No, I don't think so. I should play it safe. This means I cannot touch Austria for the time being. I should have established friendlier relations before Hitler rose to power, now it's too late."

A couple of months later

(man reads newspaper)

"Nazi propaganda is present in Austria, increasing the desire of the Austrians to join the Germans. The famous slogan of Ein Volk, ein Reich, ein Führer has appeared in many public places.

Since the Nazis are constantly rearming, while not improving their economic situation, it has appeared that they're on the brink of a collapse. First the regime of Hitler seized the assets of the Jews, then of other minorities. This move has fueled the German economy for a bit, but it's looking like it's slowing down, as the Nazis start to fall behind in the arms race with Britain and France.

Many in Nazi Germany believe that to resolve this economic issue, they shouldn't give up on their rearming efforts, but to seize Austria and Czechoslovakia. Their economies would be plundered by the Nazi regime, but it would give them an advantage in the arms race.

We know this, because today, on the 25th of January 1938, the Austrian police has raided the Vienna headquarters of the Austrian Nazi Party and arrested several key members. The Austrian police was shocked when they discovered a cache of arms and plans for a putsch."

- God damn it!

(slams table)

(door opens, door closes)

- I need to send a telegraph!
- To where, your Majesty?
- Rome.
- I'm listening.
- Hitler is looking likely he is going to invade Austria, we need to delay this as much as possible, so my troops can arrive. I will send 100,000 of my best trained men to garrison Austria and protect the country. It's going to take me around 2 months to get ready, so around the 25th of March, I should be in Austria. While the journey is only 2 weeks, I need to declare mobilization and equip the soldiers, hence the long waiting period. I don't want to send a half-equipped army. We should try to delay the invasion of Austria as by any means necessarily. Kurt Schuschnigg should meet with Hitler and perhaps give some false promises. All we need is to delay this invasion by 2 months, we should be able to do that.

(pause)

- Is that all?
- Yes.
- Understood, your Majesty, it will reach Rome tomorrow, so expect a reply the day after.
- Thank you!
- You're welcome, your majesty.

(door opens, door closes)

Days later

(man reads a report)

"Kurt Schuschnigg has been instructed to meet with Hitler and start the dismantling of the Austrian fortification. While this may sound like a bad deal, the fortifications will only hurt us in the long run. We built them to contain the Nazis, but if we want to reclaim Germany, we need to push across them. In a way, these fortifications also prevent us from pushing into Germany. Now that they are removed, we can secure a victory more easily.

On the 12th of February Schuschnigg and Hitler would meet in Berchtesgaden, which is only 30 miles from the border with Austria. We have instructed him to generally agree with him, but to stand his ground and not give a reason for an invasion. He shouldn't try to remove the Nazi propaganda from Vienna, nor ask Hitler to stop funding it. Will keep you updated with the situation."

(door opens, door closes)

(knocks on door)

- Ja.
- Karl, come with me, we need to go for a walk.

(silence)

(door opens, door closes)

(both men walk down the stairs)

- I wanted to ask you how is the situation regarding our army going? Are we ready to start sending troops to Austria?
- Your Majesty, right now we're on track and don't have any problems in particular. We should be in Austria on the 25th of March, as you have asked for.
- How's the morale of the soldiers?
- Not the highest I have ever seen, but they understand it's their duty, as part of the German Imperial Army. When Britain started their border war, the soldiers were energetic to defend their freedom. Let's hope that they regain their confidence and purpose after they arrive. I aimed to send 50,000 native Germans, ex-Great War soldiers and officers, and 50,000 native East African soldiers. I decided to go for a higher native German soldier count, as these soldiers would be the most determined, and the natives would follow in their footsteps.
- This sounds good, thank you.
- Do you think a war is really going to break out?
- It looks inevitable by that point. Hitler has ran out of money, so it's a race against time. What will happen first, Hitler will completely run out of

money and in a desperate attempt would invade, or we would get there first, where the Nazi regime would collapse in front of our very eyes. We shall see.
- Why don't the Italians and all of our allies send troops too? We have them ready and stationed into Northern Italy and western Hungary, but we cannot move into Austria directly.
- Why not?
- This would provoke Hitler for sure, so he would declare war.
- But isn't this what we want?
- Not under his conditions, if he initiates the conflict, he has the power to brainwash his people to believe his lies from sooner. If we defend Austria, even if he tries to invade, the Nazi regime will collapse, I'm telling you that much!

(silence)

12th of February, Berchtesgaden

- Nice to meet you Herr Schuschnigg, we have a lot to talk about. Look how similar Berchtesgaden and Vienna look, and I'm telling you that as an Austrian.
- Berchtesgaden is a beautiful city, but it doesn't remind me of home, Herr Hitler.
- Home?!?

(pause)

- Do you know where home is Herr Schuschnigg?
- No?
- Home is where you're born!

(man nods head)

- And do you know where you were born Herr Schuschnigg?
- Of course, I do.

(man smiles)

- Oh, so you know? I know Rive, many German speakers there I know! And you were born there! Now? This is controlled by the Italians, and you're complying with them? When was the last time you visited your home city?
- I don't remember, Vienna is my home now!

(man shakes head in disbelief)

- Home is where you were born, I already told you that! The Italians are using you, I will tell you that much! Austria was awarded as a protectorate to Italy after the Great War, you should know that. Just like Poland to Britain and Czechoslovakia to France. The Great Powers agreed to that in Locarno in 1925. Then they also let Germany join the League of Nations. All I'm trying to say is that you were played by the Entente and by the Italians. Germany is the only true friend of Austria, and you should join us at once!
- Herr Hitler I'm not looking for a war!
- But you shall receive one if you don't comply! – shouted Hitler

(silence)

- Herr Hitler, I want to avoid any unnecessary bloodshed. If we say that the Austrians and the Germans were to unite, how can we achieve that, without war and without bloodshed?
- We would need you to include some Nazi sympathizers into positions of power. Your people won't object to that, they already like us. I also want you to dismantle your fortifications on our shared border. Austria and Germany, a brother nation, or even the same nation, just divided, look like the border between France and Germany. This shouldn't continue! If all demands are met, I personally promise you to publicly reaffirm the treaty of the 11th of July 1936, and reaffirm my support for Austria's national sovereignty.
- I agree with these terms, dismantling of the fortifications would begin immediately, with your Nazi supporters being granted their position of power. Send me a letter later of who you want.
- Pleasure working with you, my Aryan brother!

(both men shake hands)

(door opens, door closes)

Days later

(man reads newspaper)

"Austria and Nazi Germany come to terms. Crisis is adverted! Nazi Germany will not attack their southern neighbor.

Both Adolf Hitler and Kurt Schuschnigg met in Berchtesgaden, a city 30 kilometers from the Austrian border. There after intense negotiations, both sides were able to come to terms. Schuschnigg expressed his desire to keep the sovereignty of his country, and Hitler proposed the terms for that.

They agreed that Austria should dismantle their fortifications with the German Reich, as it's ugly for two brother nations to be divided by fortifications. Nazi sympathizers would take positions of power in Austria, which would appease the pro-Nazi population of Austria.

This day shall be celebrated by every German-speaker, as a war between two brother nations was adverted. Long live the Germanic culture!"

(silence)

- Did we, do it? I think we managed to avoid the crisis.
- How come Hitler just decided to abandon his claims of uniting the German people?
- Either he is scared, or he realizes the situation.
- But why would he give up?
- I think that he would appoint economic ministers in Austria, as they agreed to Nazi sympathizers to get positions of power. Austria would simply become a German puppet, with Schuschnigg as a figurehead, but war would be avoided. Hitler would secure gains from the Austrian treasury with this move, he has no reason to invade.
- Or army was already sent and sailing towards Europe, do we return them? Austria is still in a crisis, but it looks like we need to resolve it diplomatically, not militarily.

- Retreat the army, we're not in the best economic situation either, but unlike Hitler, we don't have any neighbors we can bully into submission.

(laugher)

- Good night, your Majesty!
- Good night, Karl!
- We really did save Austria with this one!
- Gott mit uns!

You want a battle, here's a war!

- Have you seen this one? Let me show you.

(man hand another man a newspaper cutout)

"Arthur Seyss-Inquart was appointed as Minister of Public Security in Austria, which gave him, and in turn the Nazis, unlimited control of the police. Some violent tactics of the Austrian Nazis were opposed and suppressed."

- That's interesting, the Nazis are actually working and helping Austria. I guess they will just steam their economy. The Austrians are still obeying the Rome Protocols, and Kurt Schuschnigg is still the Austrian Chancellor.

The next day

(man hand another man a newspaper)

- Your majesty, if I were you, I'd stop everything that I'm doing and thinking about and read this. You know where to find me after that.

(man picks up newspaper)

"On the 20th of February, Hitler made a speech before the Reichstag. This speech was not only heard in Germany, but in Austria too, as it was broadcast live by the Austrian radio network. A key phrase in the speech was aimed at the Germans living in Austria and Czechoslovakia. It was: The German Reich is no longer willing to tolerate the suppression of ten million Germans across its borders."

- These damn Germans! They have not kept their word, and we fell for it! Our army is on the way home, telling them to return back to Italy would demoralize them more, but we have to do it. We will also re-shuffle the

troops being sent, with some staying here this time, and others being sent to fight. This time if Germany doesn't declare war, we will!
- With that tempo, we can have an army in Austria by the 31st of March, of not later, your Majesty.
- It has to be done, anything must be done to prevent an Austrian collapse!

Weeks later

- Your majesty, a telegraph from the Kingdom of Italy has arrived.

(man reads printed out paper)

"On 3 March 1938, Austrian Socialists offered to back Schuschnigg's government in exchange for political concessions. Austria may erupt in a civil war if the Nazis find out about this possible cooperation.

Schuschnigg agreed to these demands and was supported by the united front of socialists and communists, as well as the majority of the Austrian police.

Kurt Schuschnigg has decided to enact a referendum, where the socialists would support Schuschnigg's government, in exchange for their promised concessions.

On the 11th of March, Adolf Hitler threatened with an invasion of Austria. He demanded that Chancellor Schuschnigg resign and in his place the appointment of Arthur Seyss-Inquart.

A referendum regarding the future of Austria was called for the 13th of March due to rioting Austrian Nazis in Vienna. If this wasn't done, Austria would have erupted in a civil war, but a German invasion now looks imminent. I hope that with this move, we will have enough time for your army to arrive. Your Imperial Army will arrive in Austria two or three weeks after the referendum has ended. We should delay the results too, so there is a chance you can reach us in time."

- Will we make it in time?

- Probably not...

(silence)

- Do you have any ideas on how to delay the outcome?
- Your Majesty, if I were in Schuschnigg's shoes, I would release all the prisoners and tell them to burn Vienna, so the Nazis don't get anything of value.

(silence)

- I will ask Mussolini to start evacuating the Austrian treasury. I want an update on the situation from every 4 hours. Ask Rome about that!
- Yes, your Majesty!

(door opens, door closes)

The next day

- Your majesty, your update of the situation in Austria.
- Danke.

"To secure a large majority in the referendum, Schuschnigg dismantled the one-party state. Social democrats and communists have started to gain power in Austria, which are a big counterweight to the Nazi ideology. The minimum age for the referendum was set to 24 years, as we recognize that most young people are pro-Nazi and pro-unification. The opposite was done by Hitler in 1935, when he lowered the voting age, so more young Nazis would vote for him.

Tomorrow the people will vote regarding the future. We are optimistic that we would get a majority for pro-independence. The communists and socialists alone make around 35% of the vote. In addition, we have our loyalists and Christian parties.

This way, the world will see that the Austrian people want independence and even if Hitler were to invade, France and Britain would stop him. This is a clear violation of the treaty of Versailles, and France and Britain know it! The world is watching the situation in Austria closely"

(silence)

- There is no way that the Nazis declare war, this would be too irresponsible on their part, right? They know our army is on the way, and the Italians are on the border. I think that the same situation of 1934 is repeating itself, where Hitler tried to coup Austria, but the Italians protected them.

(silence)

"This is it... The Germans are just testing our alliance, they want to see how united we are. So far, we haven't; disappointed, I think" – thought to myself.

- I'm hoping the next message from Rome is even more positive. This is the beginning of the end of the Nazi regime in our Homeland! Gott mit uns!

4 hours later

- Your majesty, another update regarding the situation in Austria.
- Danke!

"Your Majesty, to our intelligence it has appeared that Hitler will not sit idle while the Austrians vote for their independence. Hitler has declared in a private setting that the referendum would be subject to major fraud and that the Nazis would never accept it.

In addition, the Nazi ministry of propaganda has issued a report to their public. It states that riots had broken out in Austria and that large parts of the Austrian population were calling for Nazi troops to restore order. It looks like many Nazi residents are falling for this, as they believe the Nazi regime is the savior, not the conqueror. We're in close communication with the French, as they're also monitoring the situation closely."

(man drops glass)

(it hits the floor and breaks)

(silence)

(door opens, door closes)

4 hours later

(man lights cigar)

"Hitler had sent an ultimatum to Schuschnigg, demanding that he hand over all power to the Austrian Nazis or face an invasion. The ultimatum would expire at noon, so by the time this reaches you, it has expired. Austria mobilized its soldiers, who are loyal to the Popular Front of Austria and Kurt Schuschnigg. The police are also overwhelmingly on our side. Even if there is a possible incursion into Austrian territory, we and our allies will hold until your arrival.

The Austrian military was instructed with abandoning the western Alps, which includes the major city of Innsbruck. Salzburg would also be abandoned. We will focus on defending the majority of the population to the east of the country, which includes Vienna, Graz, and Klagenfurt am Wörthersee."

(man puffs on cigar)

(silence)

"In the confusion of the invasion, we will pray that the French would also join the invasion, or send their own ultimatum. Edgar Ansel Mowrer is an award winning journalist, who has reported from Paris that: There is no one in all France who does not believe that Hitler would invade Austria just so they don't hold a genuine plebiscite. This would prevent Schuschnigg from demonstrating to the entire world just how little hold National Socialism really had on Austria.

The French have not started their mobilization efforts, but they acknowledge the danger and their public is aware of the situation. It's more than likely that we will fight on the frontlines, while France puts diplomatic pressure on Germany.

So far, the situation isn't hopeless, but Schuschnigg had to flee to Italy, so he avoids capture. This would make the logistics of the Nazis seizing power more difficult, and in turn, more time consuming."

(man puffs on cigar)

(silence)

4 hours later

(man lights cigar)

"Since Schuschnigg has left Austria, Seyss-Inquart has proclaimed himself as Chancellor, but this is not recognized by the constitution. When Seyss-Inquart tried to send a telegram to the Nazis, asking for German troops, it failed to gain legitimacy.

On the morning of 12 March 1938, the 8th Army of the German Wehrmacht crossed the border into Austria."

(pause)

(silence)

(relights cigar)

"On the morning of 12 March 1938, the 8th Army of the German Wehrmacht crossed the border into Austria. The troops were greeted in Salzburg by cheering Austrians with Nazi salutes, Nazi flags, and flowers.

The Austrian police started resisting, but unfortunately, they were slaughtered in the regions where the Austrian army was not present."

(silence)

"We think that Salzburg has fallen, with many more bordering regions soon to fall. The Austrian Army still hasn't been tested in action. Italian and

Hungarian troops are crossing into Austria and setting up defensive positions.

We have no intel on what France and Britain are planning."

4 hours later

(knocks on door)

- Ja?

(door opens, door closes)

- I'm surprised you're not asleep, your majesty.
- How could I...
- You know you have to go there personally. You better have a goodnight's sleep.
- I will sleep on the way there. Do you have the report?

(man hands another man paper)

(door opens, door closes)

(man reads newspaper)

"Hitler personally crossed the border to see his birthplace, Braunau am Inn, with a 4,000 man bodyguard. In the same evening, he arrived at Linz, where he was welcomed. It has been reported that the Nazis didn't expect this warm welcome, truly everybody was shocked to see it. Prior to that, it as thought that the Austrian people opposed uniting with Germany.

Seyss-Inquart was proclaimed as the new Austrian Chancellor, with the western part of the country becoming a German client state. Kurt Schuschnigg returned to Vienna, where he would continue ruling the Federal State of Austria. The country is in a state of civil war. The Nazis still haven't reached our armies, so we don't know how either we or they would perform."

- God...

"Social Democrats and communists were given position of power in the remainder of Austria. If this is not done, they would rebel and we would for sure lose Austria. If that were to happen and the conflict continues, Hungary would also easily fall.

There is still no former declaration of war among us. We will vote on weather we should declare war, as per Protocol No. 1 of the Rome protocols. So far, the Kingdom of Italy is in support of declaring war, the Kingdom of Hungary is in support of declaring war, the Albanian Kingdom is in support of declaring war, but the Tsardom of Bulgaria has abstained.

We have promised them future rights to Yugoslavia, but they're not budging. It's looking likely that the Bulgarians would leave the Rome protocols.

The Little Entente is also mobilizing, but not against us. They want to protect Czechoslovakia from future German aggression. Our factions are in a direct opposition and our participating nations are claiming each other's lands."

- I must go and arrive as soon as possible. If I go by plane, I can arrive just when my soldiers do, which would be in a bit over 2 weeks.

(man gets up from the chair)

(door opens, door closes)

The next day

- Gather everyone, we have big news! Two weeks ago, we sent your best troops to protect Austria from Nazi expansion! Today it has been announced that the Kingdom of Italy and the Kingdom of Hungary have declared war on the German Reich, with Austria being split in half and in an active state of a civil war. The German Empire in Exile must defend our Austrian brothers from this unfair fate that is brought upon them. We declare war on the German Reich!

(crowd cheer)

(loud noises)

- Gott mit uns!
- Gott mit uns! – the crowd shouted back!
- We shall reclaim our homeland in Europe, dismantle the Nazi regime, and imprison those responsible for crimes against humanity and the invasion of Austria. Long live the German Empire!

(crowd cheer)

18 days later

(man reads papers)

"The Nazi client state in Austria has around 1.5 million people under its control, with us having the rest of 6.6 million, which is 5.1 million. Austrian cities under Nazi occupation are: Dornbirn and the whole Vorarlberg region in general, Worgl, Maria Alm, Zell, am See, Schadming, Hallstatt, Steyr, and Freistadt. Everything north of these cities is occupied by the Nazis. This includes the major cities of Salzburg and Linz.

Vienna is an open rebellion, as there are many Nazi sympathizers, but the socialists and communists are putting them down. Quite the opposite of what happened in Germany when Hitler rose to power, as now the Socialists and imprisoning, torturing, and executing Nazis.

Austrian soldiers are dealing with the rebels within their country, as well as eliminating pockets of resistance. Hungarian troops are tasked with holding Innsbruch, Bad Hofgastein, and Klagenfurt am Wörthersee, the whole Tyrol region in general.

Italian troops are holding the frontline against the Germans, and while there was some enemy pushing, the situation is under control. Kurt Schuschnigg will announce a the results of the referendum on the 1st of April, where the Austrians would have voted regarding whether they should join Germany or stay independent.

A case was also presented to the League of Nations, but it would most likely be ignored, just like our invasion of Ethiopia."

- And what are France and Britian doing about this?
- Your Majesty, the French and the British are currently just watching the situation unfold. In Paris there was a pro-Austrian and anti-Nazi rally, but it fails to gather any actual support.
- We need to talk to them and tell them about Versailles.
- They know that the Nazis are violating it, but they're choosing not to put any pressure from the Germans. We don't know why.
- Because they're cowards! I know they are!
- Your Majesty, since the frontlines have stalled, we would need to remind these Nazis that we're at war. We would need your troops on the frontline in Lower Austria, with the goal to capture the most populus Nazi occupied city - Linz.

(man nods head)

- This is the easy part. The hard part is to decide what we want to do with the Hungarians.
- What do you mean, Signor Mussolini?
- Hungary has requested the Austrian province of Burgenland as compensation for their efforts, and that they should receive it as soon as possible. What I'm afraid of is that Hungary can switch sides and join the Germans, who will also grant them these lands. What is best that we do is we comply with the Hungarian demands for the time being.

(silence)

- Then this would make Schuschnigg's government appear even weaker and less legitimate, correct?
- Indeed, your Majesty. Hitler can use this as a propaganda on many levels, but it can work in our favor.
- How?
- Right now, Hitler is justifying that he wants to unite all the German speakers under one. Austria is predominantly German, with the Kingdom of Italy also having some German speakers. If we give Austrian Burgenland to Hungary, Hitler will need to justify taking down another nation to achieve his goals. At some point I assume the people of Germany would realize how hopeless their situation actually is.

- Speaking of a hopeless situation, Signor Mussolini, how hasn't the German economy collapsed already? Why are they not attacking us? Aren't they desperate to take the Austrian treasury so they can save their economy?
- I think that Hitler knows we have already evacuated all the Austrian treasury, so he knows that even if he were to capture Vienna, it would be more trouble for him. The Communists and the Socialists have already seized control of the city, so we have very little influence there. Right now our headquarters are in Graz, where Schuschnigg also resides.
- Your Majesty, do you remember the cigars I gave you the first time we saw each other?
- H. Upmann? Yes, why?
- The story, your Majesty...

(silence)

- A German goes far away from home, but he always wants to return.

(man nods)

- Your Majesty, we can use this as propaganda on the Austrian people. Schuschnigg is unpopular and the monarchist faction is getting more powerful. Right now they're not considering a Hohenzollern to be on the throne, but if you achieve a military success and pledge allegiance to the Austrian people... I don't know, I'm just saying that something could work out.
- This can help against the communist opposition in Vienna, but it's too risky. Tomorrow I will enter Austria with my army, so we need to make sure everybody knows that and they praise the Kaiser.

(man nods)

- Good luck tomorrow!
- Danke!

(door opens, door closes)

The next day

(man writes on a piece of paper)

"Tomorrow I'm planning to start an assault over Linz. The city is the biggest one in German occupied Austria, so it's going to be a big blow to their legitimacy. My plan is to distract them elsewhere before I move to take Linz.

The city itself is a railway hub, so if I manage to take it, most of north Austria would fall. This would allow us to cut of the region of Upper Austria completely from supply. Salzburg is going to be the biggest stronghold…"

(man pours liquid into glass)

"I think I should attack them initially near Salzburg, so I can distract them. I think the Wehrmacht would chase me because they need their propaganda victory. I can keep running from city to city, which should exhaust the enemy. By the time we get to fight for Linz, they would think it's another small attack before the Imperial army moves on to the next city, but they would be wrong! This is going to be our biggest surprise."

(man writes on paper)

"First, I try to get as close as possible to Salzburg. The goal is to gather them into one big army against us, bit not engage into actual combat. Now they would be bundled together, which should make the Wehrmacht slower. Then the town Gmunden should be raided next. We need to enrage them, which is the next logical step. According to my intelligence, Gmuncen is a beautiful town in the area and many Austrians know it as a holiday resort. All we need to do is to raid the town and burn a lot of Nazi flags, nothing too much. I'm hoping that this would make the Wehrmacht impatient and enraged, so out of anger, they will commit a blunder."

(sips liquid out of glass)

(continues to write on paper)

"This is a good plan! We will just go from town to town and burn Nazi flags. The Wehrmacht will just chase us, as we will be a small and mobile army, they will never catch us. They will try to ambush us, but it won't work out.

Our idea is not to capture the place or to have a decisive battle, but to confuse the enemy. By doing this for a couple of days, the Wehrmacht will be only thinking about which city we will raid next, and not about which city we will aim to liberate. They will think about how they should set an ambush for us, not about how to reinforce Linz."

- Tomorrow I will sent an army to get close to Salzburg. But this is the first action my army will participate in. It's also the riskiest…

(pauses)

- I think I should personally command the army. This will give them more motivation, and most importantly, I can instruct them more precisely. The goal is not to win, nor to capture the city, they must know that. – I said to myself.

"Must be going crazy if I'm talking to myself already."

(silence)

(shuts off lights)

At 3 in the morning

(loud bang)

(silence)

(another loud bang)

(scream)

(silence)

(knocks on door)

- Ja?

(door opens, door closes)

- Your majesty, wake up, the Nazis know you're in Austria and they're bombing us. No real damage was dealt, they just wanted to send a message. Our intelligence has revealed that each minute a bomb will drop at the exact same place. We need to escort you out of here.
- God damn it, these damn Nazis! Why did I think it was going to be so easy?

(silence)

(man puts clothes on)

(door opens, door closes)

Hours later

- Didn't Mark Aurel write something while he was in the Alps, around the area we're standing now.
- I'm unaware of that, sir.
- Ah, forget about it.

Hours later

(crowd cheering)

- My people, Germans, African natives, and our allies... Today we're about to make history! This battle will be the first of many!

(crowd cheering)

- This is the beginning of the end of the German Reich and the Nazi regime! Hitler has done nothing but to enslave his people and start conflicts. Not only did he invade Austria, but he stole Spain, as he was the reason why the Republican Government failed. We need to get rid of this tyrant and reclaim our Homeland!

(crowd cheering)

- Long Live Kaiser!
- Long Live!

Later that day

"Dear diary, today we tried to do an incision into Salzburg, the Nazis were ill prepared, but we never reached the city. I think it was almost empty, but I decided it was not worth it to occupy a city so close to the border of the German Reich.

I realized that taking it would just result in more problems. My goal is not to take territory, but to cause distress in the Wehrmacht, so they will lose a decisive battle.

The problem is that the Germans have the air and armor advantage, while we don't. The Italians have contributed a battalion of armored vehicles, as well as air wings.

The problem of armored vehicles is the terrain, which is predominantly mountainous and in the best-case scenario it's all forests. This makes it difficult to move, but our troops are fast and mobile. These forests provide cover from enemy aircraft. We can use them to achieve my plan of going into German occupied town and burning Nazi flags.

Right now, we're in a camp and we're sitting 20 kilometers from the city. Tomorrow, I expect the Nazis to start reinforcing it. The weather looks like it's going to be cloudy, so I should take advantage of the situation.

For tomorrow I plan to move most of my army north, so I can capture another town and burn the Nazi flag, before leaving.

I think the Wehrmacht believes that tomorrow I will aim to take Salzburg, which I won't do. I will order my troops to still fight and advance towards it, but not to try and take it. We will expand the camp in the morning, so it looks like we're housing more people. The Nazis will think the main fight is going to happen is Salzburg, but it won't! The fight will happen in Gmunden. Gott mit uns!"

The next day

- Your Majesty, we're ready to leave!
- I suggest we attack Gmunden from the west. They will expect us to go from the east, if they're trying to defend the city. The eastern part is also harder to take, there is a fortification on that side. On the western side, even if we don't take the town completely, we will capture the railroad. We should sabotage it once we reach there!
- Yes Kaiser!
- You will command the Salzburg front, while I will head out to Gmunden.
- Yes, my Kaiser, good luck, may God be with you!

Later that day

"Dear diary, today was a bad day. I personally led 1000 men to their death. The campaign in Gmunden ended in a total disaster.

The Nazi scums were waiting for us, as if they knew when and where we were going to attack. I think it was my mistake, as I chose to attack from the western side. The problem with that is that the western side is in between two lakes, Lake Attersee and Lake Traunsee.

There is a big possibility that since the western way around Lake Traunsee is closer to the German border, and the relative lack of forests, that the Germans saw our army marching and were able to send reinforcements.

We completely failed our objective and did not enter the town. We were met by resistance at Altmünster, 3 kilometers before the goal of Gmunden.

I think that I underestimated the enemy, or my doctrine and tactics are outdated. As much as I hate the Nazis, their militaristic state knows how to fight! They're perfectly combining tanks and air support, their artillery attacks are always accurate...

I think that this is going to be a new type of war, never seen before. The tactics of the Great War are not working out. I have no experience with thanks an air support, and cannot produce any, even under license. Only my Italian allies have experience with it, but their numbers are smaller, compared to the ones of the Wehrmacht.

Tomorrow I will try an assault around Salzburg again, where I will link up all my forces. I was already defeated around the Lakes east of the city, so I want to try an assault from the west. This would include going into core-Nazi German land, for the first time in 19 years some of my troops, generals, officers, and myself included will step in and touch the motherland!

I remember tearing up even when our train passed through the Italian Alps. I could feel the energy of the German speakers there, it really made me love my country even more. I cannot imagine what it would be like tomorrow when we will attempt to cross into Nazi territory.

Before we do that, I will task my soldiers with taking the town of Unken, which I hope to turn into a regional supply hub. If this is successful, I can take the city of Berchtesgaden, where Hitler and Kurt Schuschnigg met 2 months ago, where they agreed for the Austrian state to remain independent, under Hitler's conditions.

Taking this city would be a massive victory, as it would open up the way for Salzburg. We can attack it from the east already, and if all of this succeeds, we can also attack it from the west and south.

I want to leave the north free. This is because I don't want to encircle the Nazis, I think this will lead to our downfall. When you encircle an army, they know they will be fighting to the last man, so they fight fearlessly. What I have noticed over the years is that if you leave them an opening, they will escape, rather than to fight until they're dead.

The offense on Linz is paused, but I will return to it after I cross into mainland Germany first, so I can get the morale of my troops high.

If the people in Berchtesgaden accept me, this would give me legitimacy and we can say that the Kaiser has returned to the German homeland, to liberate the people from oppression and tyranny."

(shuts off light)

The next day

(gunshot sound, one after another)

(artillery fire)

(the ground vibrates)

(dirt is thrown everywhere)

- Kaiser, we cannot push them! They have fortified the surrounding mountains and are using artillery fire, and they are pretty damn good at that!

(artillery shell falls hundreds of meters away)

(loud bang)

- Kaiser, this is a meat grinder, our troops have no chance. They have the terrain advantage. We need to attempt these tactics again on flat terrain, preferably on our terms. We cannot achieve a breakthrough! We need to pull back!

(man nods)

4 hours later

(man writes on telegram)

"What is going on with France and Britian, do we have an answer? A couple of days ago I lost 1000 soldiers, today I lost 2500 more. I have already lost 7% of the army I sent to Austria. I have thousands more wounded and are unfit to fight for the time being.

I want to open up a new front. Our relations with Czechoslovakia are not the best, but I can go there and talk to them, or even go to Paris and talk with the French. Unless somebody joins this war, we might not live to see its end!"

1 hour later

"Your Majesty, the war has turned against us. Today the Wehrmacht started their advance to Vienna from Linz. The cities of Stayr and Amstetten have officially fallen to the Nazis. They're going along the Danube River, so their supply lines are vulnerable.

I suggest instead of going to Paris or Prague to negotiate, first we take an opportunity at this encirclement."

(silence)

(door opens, door closes)

- I would need a detailed map of Lower Austria.
- Wait a minute, your Majesty.

(silence)

(man lights cigar)

- There you go. Here is also a pencil.
- Danke!

(door opens, door closes)

"Here I am, again alone with my thoughts."

(puffs on cigar)

"I need to learn from the enemy and organize an ambush. They're going along the Danube towards Vienna. Amstetten has fallen... Where is it again?"

(pause)

"Ah, there it is. So, the Nazis are halfway Vienna. The town of Melk looks to be on the Danube, and is also hallway from Amstetten to Vienna. We can send an army there. To the north of the river there is a mountainous terrain, we can hide artillery in there. I don't have artillery, but will request some from the Italians.

Schönbühel an der Donau, it's only 3 kilometers away from Melk, I want to station troops there too. I aim for the Germans to pass through Melk and meet our army at Schönbühel an der Donau. Then the forces we hid in the hills north of Melk would come out, and we would also need forces from the south. This should completely encircle the German divisions and we will just destroy them with artillery. This should work, I don't see a way that it doesn't.

It doesn't matter if the Germans send tanks our way or not, we will just encircle the armored vehicles. The air situation wouldn't also matter. We cannot spare any air wings, so we will not fight on air. The enemy cannot bomb our positions, they can only try in Schönbühel an der Donau. The rest of the army would be safe.

What would happen is that even if they send tanks and planes our way, we will encircle the tanks and the air won't spot the army hiding in Melk and the surrounding hills. They will just bomb where they think we are.

This will work! Gott mit uns!"

The next day

- Attention everyone! The Kaiser is going to tell you his plan.
- Danke.

(clears throat)

- The Hungarians should make their way to Schönbühel an der Donau, where they will expect to be attacked by the Germans, considering that they continue following the Danube, going towards Vienna. The Austrian army should continue pacifying the countryside. We have almost cleared the rebellions, but we don't want Austrian soldiers to fight currently. I believe that this would give the Nazis more propaganda, so they will intensify their bombings of Vienna and Linz.
- What about us?
- The Italians should continue their hold on Tyrol but can pretend like they're advancing forwards and abandoning Innsbruch. This should

create more confusion in the German army, allowing for the main front to succeed. They cannot concentrate and make unanimous decisions if we confuse them enough.

(people nod head)

(people start clapping)

- What about the Nazi tanks and planes? We cannot rival them.
- All is going to work, it's a solid plan, that should neglect the armor and air advantage of the enemy. Once we encircle the Nazis in Melk and Schönbühel an der Donau, no armor and air can help them break free. The best way to approach these kinds of battles is to avoid the advantage of the enemy. I believe I have found their advantage. We should act quickly, and after that I will head to Prague and Paris, so I can negotiate with the Allies and the Little Entente regarding a possible terms for intervention.

(people start applauding the Kaiser)

The next day

- Listen soldiers, the Kaiser won't participate in this operation, as he would try to secure foreign support for our war against the Nazis. I will be leading you.
- Yes, Marshal Mackensen! – said all the soldiers unanimously.
- We should make a camp around there.

(man points at a hill)

- On the hill we would have clear vision over Melk, but due to the tree density, the enemy aircraft wouldn't spot us. We would set up outposts 100 meters from each other, so we're not concentrated into one spot. After I give you signal, we would charge at the enemy. We should strike them from behind, so we would catch them off guard. The chances of them surrendering after that are quite high!
- Yes commander! – The soldiers shouted!

2 hours later

- Marshal von Mackensen, we have received news that the Wehrmacht is approaching Melk. We should start see German soldiers occupying Melk, then they would continue forward.
- Good, stay in position.

(man looks though his binoculars)

- Ha! I see them! They look to be marching slowly and on the main road, what are they doing? What a shame we're lacking artillery to shred these bastards to pieces.

(silence)

- There is no armor support…

(silence)

- And I haven't heard an aircraft flying over us. We're on the clear!

(pause)

- Sargent, do you know what is that yellow building over there, it looks gorgeous! Here, have a look.

(man looks through the binoculars)

- Hm… looks like a monastery, not necessarily a church. All the sculptures are of women it looks like. Could be an Abbey.
- Is it the Baroque style? This is something special!
- I'm unaware, Marshal, sorry.
- Ah, forget about that, get in position, soon we would have the signal to attack from Schönbühel an der Donau.
- Yes, Marshal!

30 minutes later

- The enemy has just successfully occupied Melk, the citizens look to be confused... as of they don't know we're at war.

(spits on ground)

- They're searching for an army, cannot find anything. They seem to be in disbelief that we let such a beautiful town fall.
- I see Wehrmacht soldiers raiding the train station. They seem to be taking a couple of people hostage.

(silence)

- I think that they're just jews, trying to flee the Nazi regime.

(distant gunshot sound)

(silence)

(distant gunshot sound again)

(both men look at each other in disbelief)

- Killing civilians? These guys are clearly violating many international treaties. I don't want to know what it would look like to be a prisoner of war to these guys.
- Ha, you think they're taking prisoners.

(silence)

- Maybe that's why they're being so effective at defeating us so far? They just don't play by the rules.
- Could explain a lot.

(silence)

- Hey, look there!
- What are these bastards doing in the Abbey?

(gunshot)

(gunshot)

- No!
- These bastards!
- Shup up, don't make noise!
- I'm going to kill you! – shouted the man on top of his lungs.

(gunshots stop)

- I think they may have heard you!
- You think so? They're about 500 meters away.
- If they stopped what they were doing, then yes.
- But they don't know we're here, and they don't know we're soldiers. It could have been anyone, right?
- Right…

(silence)

- God have mercy on the souls whose lives were taken away today…
- Look, they're moving past the town, they're advancing towards the Hungarians.
- Quick, go listen to the radio, we need to know whether we should attack!

Minutes later

- The Wehrmacht and the Hungarian army have just started exchanging shots 500 meters from Schönbühel. We can strike them from behind.
- I was monitoring the situation in Melk closely, there are around a hundred Nazis stationed there. Once we appear with a thousand strong army, they will surrender I bet! First order is to take back Melk, then the Nazi soldiers that advanced towards Schönbühel would be encircled.
- I will prepare the soldiers.

(man gets off the ground, walks away)

10 minutes later

"I can see my soldiers cross the bridge into Melk. There were 5 Nazi soldiers guarding it. It appears like they were caught of guard. One drops his cigarette on the ground. All kneel down. Good. They have surrendered.

Not a single shot was fired, unless the Nazis in Melk were looking at them, they won't expect what's about to come upon them next. If my officers are smart, they will not send all the soldiers at once through the bridge, but 5 at once. To the enemy, it would appear that the same 5 that guarded the bridge are just patrolling, not that we're flowing soldiers in."

(silence)

"If it takes 1 minute for 5 soldiers to cross, in an hour that would be 300. We would need to be here over 3 hours just to cross the troops safely.

There are only around a hundred enemy troops in Melk. We can wait 20 minutes, then I will order an attack from all sides, and all 900 people would cross simultaneously, while the 100 that have already crossed would cause chaos."

(pauses)

"Yes, this would work. 20 minutes, no more. The Hungarians should have an easy time holding, but not to beat them so much that the Wehrmacht decides to retreat into our trap."

20 minutes later

"Time!"

(radio buzz)

- Sargent, order all your troops to cross, and the ones that have crossed should attack the Nazi positions!

(radio buzz)

- Understood!

(silence)

- There they go!

"The Nazis have surrendered the train stationed. The bodies of the jews they shot are still laying on the ground, it's been an hour since they shot them... Wait, these 3 were digging a hole, maybe it's for them. Our troops have secured the Abbey.

The Imperial Army is going to be victorious against the Wehrmacht!

The town's center looks to be fallen. Civilians are confused and don't know what's going on."

(distant gunshot)

- There goes our cover.

"Now all the Nazis nearby know we're attacking Melk. I will order the Hungarians to start pushing them towards us!"

(radio buzz)

- We have secured Melk, all resistance is almost cleared out and the civilians are under control, commence your counterattack on the enemy!

(radio buzz)

- We're on it!

(silence)

"Melk is secured. I think that the Wehrmacht knows that they're encircled, they should surrender now."

(pauses)

(man pulls out a map)

"Looking at this, to their northeast is the Danube River, to their southeast we have our army at Melk, and to the northwest are the Hungarians. The enemy can only escape going southwest, and even then, they would be in open fields, not a pleasant situation to find themselves in.

If they have done their research, they will take refuge in the village of Hub. It looks like only 50 people live there. We have already won it, they fell for our trap. Even if we had artillery, we wouldn't bomb it, as we don't want the civilians to suffer.

Hub is slightly positioned on a hill, this can cause a problem, but most likely won't. The Wehrmacht should be in panic."

1 hour later

(radio buzz)

- Marshal Mackensen, as you have predicted, the Wehrmacht has taken refuge in Hub. All roads leading outside of the city have been cut off from supply, we control the area. Around 3000 Wehrmacht troops are encircled, what a blow to the Nazi war effort and morale! This would be their first major defeat!
- Good, order the troops to wait and starve them. With 3000 soldiers in a village of around 50 people, they should run out in 3 days.

(vibration in the sky)

(airplane passes by)

(silence)

(sounds of many airplanes)

- What is this?

(silence)

(man looks through binoculars)

- They're dropping crates with parachutes? These bastards! Our encirclements mean nothing!

(man spits on ground)

(silence)

(radio buzz)

- Marshal Mackensen, it has appeared that the Wehrmacht is sending in tanks our way, they should be in Melk after 10 minutes. Our intelligence has counted 500 soldiers and 20 armored vehicles. Airplanes are a possibility.

(radio buzz)

- Bastards! – screamed Marchal Mackensen so loud that his throat hurt.

(radio buzz)

- I want to call for a retreat. Don't go to Melk, but to Schönbühel instead. I want you to fortify the place as quickly as possible. Leave out the encircled troops in Hub.

(radio buzz)

- Understood.

(radio buzz)

The next hour

"Wehrmacht troops have arrived in Melk and have connected with the troops that were encircled prior to our retreat. I can count 50 armored vehicles and many more soldiers. It looks like they will be more cautious in the future, but we didn't secure any gains. We just delayed their attack on Vienna.

We lost 47 men in the brawl, while the Wehrmacht lost 175. We will count that as a victory in the history books!"

The next day

- Your Majesty, I have returned from the frontlines, we successfully managed to prevent a further Wehrmacht advance along the Danube. We eliminated more soldiers than we lost. The situation is in our favor, despite the enemy's armor and air superiority.
- Good job, Marshal Mackensen! I always knew you were the man for the job!
- It has also appeared that the Wehrmacht is going to consider their every move and be more cautious in the future. This should buy us time.
- Speak to you later Marshal Mackensen. So far, the frontlines seem to be peaceful! I would say it's too peaceful. I wonder if it's the Nazis being cautious, or are they planning something?

24 hours later

- Kaiser, you must read this report.

(man places documents on table)

"Vienna has been radicalized to the breaking point. Today, on the 16th of April the Vienna commune was declared. The eastern part of the city is in an open rebellion. It was called prior to that, Red Vienna, due to the large number of Communists and Socialists there.

Now due to the absence of a strong leader of Austria, they have declared their own sate, separate from the Federal Republic of Austria and the German Reich."

- These bastards! Can Schuschnigg do something right?
- That's the problem, your majesty. Schuschnigg was shot today in Graz by socialist supporters. New news first reached Vienna, as the socialists were the first to know of the success of the assassination. This led to the rise of the Vienna Commune.

(pauses)

- The rest of the world still doesn't know about Schuschnigg's assassination, but they will find out shortly. Austria will get destabilized beyond belief. Now the only alive Austrian Chancellor would be the Nazi Arthur Seyss-Inquart, who would gather even more legitimacy. If the communist get more powerful, the civil war in Austria can become a proxy-war by 3 sides.

(silence)

- Your majesty, you should urgently go to Paris and demand that they join the war as soon as possible, or Europe would be ruled by Nazis and Communists!
- Will do... This explains the lack of action on the frontlines by the Reich.

3 days later

(French speaking)

- Your Majesty, the Prime Minister of the French nation - Paul Reynaud, is ready to receive you.
- Bonjour Monsieur Reynaud!
- Greetings your Majesty, Emperor of the Germans in exile. What brings you to beautiful Versailles?
- Versailles was beautiful, but the treaty wasn't. Even so, it should be obeyed. What president is France setting by allowing the Nazis to do as they please? Soon other nations would start renouncing their treaties too?

(man nods head)

- France is not a dictatorship, but a republic, your Majesty. We cannot do such daring actions without the support of the public. Right now, the socialist faction in France is on the brink of taking over. Their stance is against war, so if France were to join, it would mean a civil war back home. You're on your own.

(silence)

- Hitler does claim Alsace-Lorraine, right? What if he comes and declares war on the French?
- Then, your Majesty, we would be more united, the socialists won't launch a coup and etc. Also, let me mention that France is very well fortified against the Germans, any invasion is unlikely to succeed.
- What about the British, can't they support our cause?
- What is your cause exactly? Declaring war on independent country in Africa, or?

(silence)

- Have a nice day, Monsieur Reynaud!

(door opens, door slams)

On the train back home

"These damn French people, they will collapse, but not help out an old enemy, even if it means their death!

I will go back to Rome, then I can fly to Prague next, as I would need to secure an alliance, which would end the war in our favor."

2 days later

- Your Majesty, we have terrible news. Innsbruck has fallen to the Nazis. The Wehrmacht has successfully taken not only Melk, but has advanced 20 more kilometers to Sankt Pölten. Vienna is only 50 more kilometers away.
- How's the situation in Vienna?
- We have no control there, but this is not our biggest problem. Hitler and the Kingdom of Hungary are in talks of the Hungarians possibly leaving the Rome Protocols and the war altogether, while keeping Austrian Burgenland. This deal is appealing to them, so the chance of them accepting is high. What do you think we should do?

(silence)

- What about Austria, do we have a replacement Chancellor?
- Not many are volunteering to get assassinated, so the role is absent. Our only option is to make Austria a confederation of Cantons, just like Switzerland. They will govern themselves and have complete autonomy. This decentralization would allow for the territory to exist without a Chancellor being elected.
- Smart.

(silence)

- About the Hungarians, try your best to tell them not to ally with Hitler, and that together we can receive all lands that we claim. They can get Slovakia, Vojvodina, and Transylvania if our faction ends up being at war with the Little Entente. Tell them that I just spoke with the French. They're in a very unstable position, so even if we declare war on these states, the French won't intervene. This would cause a civil war back home.

A week later

(man reads newspaper)

"The Kingdom of Hungary has officially dropped out of the war, as they signed a deal with Hitler that they would get to keep Austrian Burgenland. The former allies of the Kingdom of Hungary have decided not to invade the country, as this would only stall their progress in Austria.

Regarding the Alpine country, Vienna has officially fallen to the Nazi regime, with the Socialists being crushed. The state of the Vienna Commune couldn't last even a whole month.

Hungary pulling out of the war had several implications. The sudden return of Hungarian troops back to their homeland left a gap, which the Italians and the German Empire in Exile couldn't fill in time. The city of Linz has officially fallen.

The Austrian confederation has 14.3% of all of Austria. They control the cities of Klagenfurt am Wörthersee, with the surrounding province becoming it's own canton, Spittal an der Drau and the province is formed into a canton, and finally, Bad Gastein, which has also become the capital of it's respective canton.

Constitution of the Austrian confederation is now being written, but if the Nazis continue their advance, with that speed, all of Austria would be under the Wehrmacht in under a month.

France and Britain are looking like they will not intervene, with the Little Entente being united both against the Rome Protocols and the Nazi tread.

Will the confederation of Austria get to live for another day, or would a decisive battle force them to the negotiating table?

Hitler has personally visited Graz, with him planning to visit Vienna the same week. This solidifies the Nazi control over the county and for many Austria is synonymous not with a confederation, but with the German Reich."

Intervene and steal or help and take!

Back in Nazi Germany

- Heil! Hitler is doing something that no German has ever dared to do! He will unite all the German speakers under one flag! Only he will save the Germans!

(crowd cheers)

- Trust me people, this is our only intention, to unite the Germans. We don't want more war, we don't want more conflict, we don't want colonies... But we have to fight, for the rights of the Germans! Right now, the tens of millions of Germans are divided across 10 other countries! This is unacceptable!

(crowd cheers)

- Heil!
- Heil! – the crowd repeated.
- Only he will save the Germans! What is the Kaiser doing? He fled to Africa and waited 20 years to come back, he doesn't mean anything! The people have already forgotten about him! When Germany was a monarchy, these were the darkest days in German history! We lost the most humiliating war and signed the most humiliating peace treaty! All of this must change, and nobody else than Hitler can do that for the German people!

(crowd applauds)

- This is why we must start acting now! Austria has almost been pacified! If you need any proof that our regime is superior and that national socialism will live on for a thousand years, look to Austria. They tried socialism in Vienna and couldn't last a month. They tried Italian Fascism and now control less than 14% of all Austrian lands.

(pauses)

- But the national socialists... we're clearly superior! We have resisted the enemy's efforts to invade us and push their scum ideology upon our people! Not a single enemy soldier has entered the mainland of the German Reich, but how many Wehrmacht soldiers are in Austria, right?

(crowd nods head)

- We will fight until we unite all the Germans, then we will stop and become the most peaceful nation in the world! This is all we need, a united Germany, nothing more!

(crowd cheering)

- This is why, my fellow Germans, I ask you to rebel against your Czechoslovak overlord, as you're neither Czech, nor Slovak. There is no reason for a million Germans to live here and not in Germany! Try your best efforts to resist the enemy and soon, we will send help from the Reich! Let us reunite the Sudetenland into the Reich, and the German people in Central Europe shall finally be united!

(crowd cheering)
- Heil!
- Heil Germany! – the crowd responded.
- Dear Germans, take a look at what the Czechoslovak government is doing to you right now! For 2 years they have fortified our shared border, amassing a fortress. What do you think that is for? To keep the Nazi tread away, or to keep you, my dear Germans inside?

(silence)

(people start booing the Czechoslovak republic)

(somebody lit a Czechoslovak flag on fire)

(public discontent)

The next day

(man reads newspapers)

"On the 30th of June 1938, Sudeten Nazi Konrad Henlein has sparked a revolt in Czechoslovakia. He has agitated the Germans in Czechoslovakia to openly rebel against the government.

A list of demands, also called the eight points, has been submitted to the Czechoslovak government. The Nazis say that Czechoslovakia must do these requests, so the Sudeten Germas can be equal to the Czechs.

The British have sent Lord Runciman to investigate the situation in the Sudetenland. He would meet with the Czechoslovak President Edvard Beneš and Prime Minister Milan Hodža, but also with Sudeten Germans agitated by Konrad Henlein.

So far, there are three plans to deal with the crisis that the British have proposed. First is for the German Reich to annex and integrate Czechoslovakia, the second is for the region to hold a plebiscite on which territory they should join, with the final option being for Czechoslovakia to become a federation.

Only time will tell what the Great Powers will agree to!"

(man puts down newspaper)

- Finally, some good news! These British bastards ignored Austria, but now suddenly care about Czechoslovakia. The Nazis are being stupid once again! I love the three British proposals, all of them would benefit us and neither would Nazi Germany!
- How come, your Majesty?
- If Germany directly annexes the territory, it will mean that Czechoslovakia will join our cause, Hungary is no longer in our alliance, so we can work with them.
- What about the Little Entente?
- What about them? Do you really think that the Romanian and Yugoslav Army is going to stay in the conflict long enough, or will they drop out just like Hungary, while securing something from the Reich?

(pauses)

- The allies of Czechoslovakia will abandon them, but we won't! We're fighting for the same cause! Maybe it's about time for us to go to Prague and speak with Beneš, while also announcing our goals and not claiming any Czechoslovak land directly.
- What about the other points?
- Plebiscite in the region would benefit us the most. I'm hoping for the same situation as in Austria to happen, this will for sure make the Great Powers intervene and secure our victory.
- How come?
- If the situation with Austria repeats, the plebiscite would be against joining the Reich. The Nazis won't accept that, so they would invade, before waiting for it to end. This will open a massive, truly massive frontline, that is across flat terrain. This will overstretch the Germans, Czechoslovakia just doesn't need to give up!
- And third? How does that help us?
- Czechoslovakia becoming a federation would mean less power for the cowardly President Edvard Beneš. We can get the Czechs on our side and secure that they join the Rome Protocols instead. Most importantly, it would weaken the German justification for uniting the German speakers. It would be a big blow for the Nazi ideology.

Days later

(man reads newspaper)

"Czechoslovakia announces their intent to transition to a federal type of governance. The country is currently working on a new constitution, that would appeal to the Sudeten Germans and to the British demands.

We know that the country will become called: Federation of Central Europe, as the name Czechoslovakia ignores the millions of Germans, and hundreds of thousands of Hungarians, Ruthenians, and Poles, living within the nation's borders.

A federation will save Czechoslovakia's territorial integrity, and most likely avoid a Nazi invasion. A future conflict was just resolved, but Central Europe is still in flames! The conflict between the German Reich and the German Empire in Exile, together with their ally of the Kingdom of Italy, still is ongoing, with hundreds of soldiers dying on the frontlines each day.

The Allied powers of France and Britain seem uninterested to put an end to that conflict. It's evident that they want to see both sides bleed their resources away, or they have signed a secret treaty with the Nazis as to not intervene. Only time will tell us the truth, which always comes out sooner or later!"

(man lights a cigar)

- Well, we didn't get lucky with this one, but maybe we can still get the Czech side of the federation to join us. I bet that the Czechs are radicalized at this new change. They used to be the masters of their own country and now would have to share power with Poles, Germans, and Hungarians. This is a big blow to Czech nationalism, they will soon come looking for us!

(pause)

- Your Majesty, there are reports from the battlefield, today we have officially lost Bad Gastein. We officially control less than 10% of Austria's territory and only 5% of their total population. In total, we have lost 13,000 soldiers out of the 50,000 that we sent. We have 21,000 wounded, so our fighting capabilities are diminished greatly. I will request 50,000 more soldiers from East Africa, and return the wounded.

(man nods)

- These Nazis, they're unfair! The Allies know that the Nazis are killing civilians are committing all kinds of crimes but are refusing to acknowledge that! I don't know what's the bid deal between these two sides. I think that they're working together... Then why wouldn't they help us?

(silence)

- Bastards!

The next day

- Your Majesty, have you read the news today?
- No, I don't read them without you!

(laugher)

(man hands newspaper to another man)

"Hitler is outraged at the new state borders of the Central European Federation. He has officially said: The Sudetenland is the last territorial demand I have to make in Europe. Many believe this to be true, and after this is awarded to Germany and they receive all of Austria, only then peace can be secured in Austria.

Czechoslovakia is resisting that, however, and this shows in their new state borders. There is no Sudeten state, but the Germans are mixed with Czechs. The state borders are drawn in such a way that doesn't give the Germans a majority in any state.

This has seen by the Nazi leadership as a great tread to the German people. They have openly claimed that they want to annex this territory."

(man puts down newspaper)

- If all goes well, we will have our army ready when the Germans cross into Czechoslovakia. We will join our efforts and defeat the Nazis. The war can be soon over!
- What about the Kingdom of Italy?
- What about them?
- Don't you think they will drop out of this war?
- No, why would they?
- They have already lost tens of thousands of soldiers too, and without anything to show for it. Public unrest in the Kingdom is growing about this Mussolini guy. People have begun calling for an absolute monarchy.
- Mussolini will never sign a peace treaty. This would mean that he admits to his people that he has lost the war, which will most likely result in him

losing power. He loves power, he will do everything to assure he's in power, even if it means that the Nazis would have to chase him to Sicily!

The next day

(man turns on radio)

- Seeing that the Czechoslovaks will not cooperate, the German Reich has requested a cession of the Sudetenland, which was agreed to by France and Britain. This allows the Nazi leadership and troops to walk into the Sudetenland freely. This would allow for order to be restored, until a better solution can be found.

(radio buzz)

(silence)

- These idiots! They allowed them to enter Czechoslovakia unopposed! This is a repeat of the situation in Austria! They will radicalize the population and most likely demand a plebiscite, which they will win!
- Your Majesty, as far as I know, this decision was allowed by France and Britain, as they want to avoid any future wars. It was taken without the approval of the Czechoslovak President.
- I think that this will finally make Czechoslovakia flip to our side! Schedule a meeting in Prague right away! I must be alone, don't invite Mussolini, the Czechs don't like him!
- I'm on it, your Majesty.

The next day

- Welcome to Prague, your Majesty, how do you find the city?
- This is my first time being here, it's got good architecture, remind me of home!

(silence)

(both men walk into a building)

(door opens, door closes)

- What did you come to discuss with me?
- President Beneš, I come here to offer my help in case of a future war with Germany. I know that relations between the Rome Protocols and the Little Entente are poor, but if we don't settle our differences, we would all be under Nazi occupation.

(man nods)

(pours liquid into two glasses)

- So, what do you suggest?
- I want to disband the Rome Protocols and form a new alliance, that would benefit us both. I don't think that the Kingdom of Romania and the Kingdom of Yugoslavia are going to come to their aid, as they only issued a diplomatic objection and haven't started their mobilization efforts, unlike you and me.
- Correct.
- France and Britain look to be unreliable allies for your nation. They allowed the Germans, without your consent to enter the Sudetenland unopposed. While this is still part of your country, if there is a vote tomorrow, it would change that. The Nazis know how to manipulate the people. They will convince them to join the Reich, if the vote looks like it's not going to pass, they will simply invade. They're always getting what they want.
- What are you suggesting?
- We need to settle some key differences, if we want to establish future cooperation, or perish in the Nazi tread.

(man nods)

- Do you, and your people, support of me becoming the Kaiser of the Germans once the Nazi tread has been eliminated?
- We don't see a problem in that, as long as we sign a couple of treaties and guarantees.
- Such as?

- A non-aggression pact, a free trade agreement, and you renounce your claims on the Sudetenland and Austria.
- I think that we can work with that. What's next? Is Czechoslovakia going to remain a federation after the war?
- I want to establish the Federation of Central Europe, which would include Austria, but since you don't claim that I assume it's not going to be a problem.

(silence)

- What about Mussolini? He wanted a protectorate in Austria.
- He is not contributing enough to the war effort, your Majesty. The Czechoslovak nation has more people mobilized than the entirety of the Kingdom of Italy, and we're not at war. I don't know the plan of the Italians, but it looks to me like your soldiers are holding the frontl ne, not the Italians.

(silence)

- Still, the Italians may not respond kindly to Austria going to your domain, which would result in another war. President Beneš, if you're looking to abandon Yugoslavia to their fate, we can work with that!
- No! They're our Slavic brothers!
- But they're not supporting you in your upcoming war, correct?

(silence)

- President Beneš, the Little Entente was formed against the Hungarians, and Romania and Yugoslavia have are not threatened by the Germans, yet, so they have no need to support you. I can have Germany, you can have Austria, and Italy can have Yugoslavia. This is the only arrangement I see that could work. If not, we will get attacked by the Germans, and France and Britain will not help us, as you can see. We're truly on our own!
- France pledged to support the Little Entente when it was created!
- They did, but are they doing a good enough job by letting the Nazis into your territory?

(silence)

- Your Majesty, you're asking me to abandon my ally.
- All I'm saying is to leave them to the Italians, you don't have to join any war. We can ally, our great nations. The communists are growing stronger, Spain was in a civil war, we can be next!
- I need time to think about it.
- You don't need more time, you need more information, what do you want to know, so I can tell you while I'm here?
- Does Mussolini know about this?
- Not yet, but I assume he won't object to Yugoslavia.

(silence)

- Your majesty, do you have a plan for action?
- Tomorrow morning, or as soon as possible, you should sign a decree to form the Federation of Central Europe and ask for the Nazis to leave your territory, or face war. Your frontline with the Germans is very long and easy to defend. Many fortifications still haven't been dismantled.
- But won't the Allies object to this? After all, they signed an agreement with them that they can enter the territory.
- They just want to give away your land and secure peace. They believe it when Hitler said that it's going to be his last territorial request in Europe. This is hypocritical, as he wants to unite the German speakers. There are Germans in Lithuania, Poland, France, Switzerland and so on. What makes you think that after the Sudetenland he would have fulfilled his goals of uniting the Germans? Don't believe their lies, force them to leave!
- And what if they refuse to leave?
- You will exercise authority over your own land and send in the army to force the Nazis across the border, it is your right as a sovereign nation. In fact, if you don't do that, the Czechoslovak public might ask you to resign. They need a strong leader right now.
- And what if they declare war.
- Good! This will finally show to the world the Nazis true colors! After the Olympics in Berlin, the world was sold that this new Nazi ideology is

nothing bad. Germany attacking two independent nations in a year would show otherwise.
- Tomorrow I will mobilize all the army and send them to restore order in the Sudetenland!
- Good!

(men shake hands)

(door opens, door closes)

The next day

(man writes on paper)

"Dear diary, I'm optimistic for today. The Czechs will finally do the right thing and push the Nazi aggressors out. France and Britian will object to that, but there is nothing they can do.

The situation in Austria is bad, as Mussolini and the Italian army are barely doing anything to try and change that. I have never seen such incompetent people!

I plan for a great encirclement in Austria, which was also given to the Czechoslovak soldiers. We plan to cut Austria in half, then take the eastern part, where Vienna is located.

It's going to be easy for the Czechoslovak soldiers to push, as they will fight in forests, while we will fight in mountains. Linz is only 30 kilometers from the Czechoslovak border, which would work out in our favor. There are no other main railroad connections to Vienna once Linz has fallen. If the Czechoslovaks are swift, they can use their airplanes to bomb the remainder of the railroads.

After this is completed, I plan to go on the offense, but not in Austria. I'm going directly to Berlin, which is 200 kilometers from the Czechoslovak border!

On the way there we will occupy Saxony, where I hope the Germans in there would flip and support our cause! They might after they realize the truth of the Nazi regime!

I'm staying next to the radio, awaiting to hear the news of Czechoslovakia resisting the Germans. Gott mit uns!"

5 hours later

(radio buzz)

"Europe is on the verge of another war! The Czechoslovak President Edvard Beneš has decided not to obey the treaty between France, the United Kingdom, and the German Reich, and has sent their soldiers to escort the unwelcome Nazis out of their territory.

This was well received by the German political parties and important figures, who have taken refuge in Czechoslovakia. They said that due to the Nazi regime, their freedom and lives were at risk, so they escaped to the Sudetenland. After that became part of Nazi Germany, they fled to the Sudetenland.

These people are the heroes of Czechoslovakia, and maybe even the world, as they're denouncing the ideals of the Nazis. They go to every village in the Sudetenland where the Nazis have been and try to convince them not to follow this radical path.

In all of this chaos, Poland has decided to intervene and seized the port city of Danzig. It remains to be seen how the Nazis would respond to that tread!"

(silence)

(door bangs)

- Your Majesty, we have urgent news!
- Ja!

(door opens, door closes)

- The German Reich has declared war on Czechoslovakia officially. This information came in two minutes ago.
- Is any country from the Little Entente responding to that?
- So far, neither the Kingdom of Romania, nor the Kingdom of Yugoslavia have ordered a mobilization. If the Czechoslovaks were on their own, they would have collapsed without their allies getting close to joining the war.
- I guess that's their idea!

(silence)

- Take me to the army, we need to counterattack in this confusion. Time is the most important resource right now! We must act quickly!
- Yes, your Majesty, follow me!

30 minutes later

- Dear soldiers, I promised you to lead you to victory, and while it was a bumpy ride, we have secured an ally, who will aid us in the invasion of Austria! Before I tell you what we're going to do, is anyone in here from Saxony, or does he have relatives there?

(many people raise their hands)

- Good, I will not have you fighting today, but will send you to the Saxon frontline. There, you will have the chance to liberate your home city and the people you know and love, from this brutal Nazi dictatorship! Gott mit uns!
- Gott mit uns!
- Long live Kaiser!
- Long live!

(people start cheering)

- I want the soldiers that will participate ready in 20 minutes. We will strike north, as north as we can possibly go! The German army is most likely going to retreat to cover the massive front with Czechoslovakia. We need to slow them down, so the Czechoslovak soldiers can secure more gains. Time is our most important resource, remember! A soldier we slow down means that the bigger army of Czechoslovakia can advance and liberate our Homeland!

(people cheer)

- Once we have connected with the Czechoslovaks near Linz, we will move towards Berlin and end the war right here and right now!

The next day

(man writes on paper)

"Dear diary, today was the most exhausting day of my life! I'm blessed to have such a highly motivated army! We managed to cross the Alps unopposed and are now in the province of Upper Austria. The city of Graz has fallen to Italian troops, who marched on the city and found that it was garrisoned by a thousand Nazi soldiers.

The Czechoslovaks are holding the northern front against the Germans, waiting for us, and have started two offensives. One is to cut Silesia off, and the other is to reach Linz. We have received reports that they're 20 kilometers from the city. The Czechoslovak army decided to go along the Danube and advance on the city from two sides.

What they found is absolutely horrifying. The Czechoslovak army advanced towards the city of Mauthausen, but they found it already in flames. It was confirmed that the Czechoslovaks didn't bomb it prior to that, so they investigated.

They have found out that the Nazis set fire to it themselves and abandoned it. I was told that the Nazis set up a forced labor camp, where people deemed undesirable to them were sent there to work until their death.

We don't have concrete proof of that, but our allies found thousands of bodies wearing prison uniforms. The concentration site was also built next to a granite mine, so we can assume what was happening there. Soon, the truth would be revealed, all reports were also sent the United Kingdom and France."

The next day

"Dear diary, in two days, I believe we have created the biggest encirclement in human history. The rest of Lower Austria is completely cut off from supply. Tomorrow we will advance towards the German mainland and liberate Saxony. The Czechoslovaks have already cut Silesia in half and are bombarding the Nazi troops stationed there.

They were well received, as news of the forced labor camp reached all around the world. France is declaring mobilization, as the people demand war.

I expect the Italians to take control of Austria, while we go towards Berlin. Our representatives would meet with the French, regarding a possible peace deal. They might also soon become partners in the war, so we need to know their goals.

It's important for us that we agree on me, the Kaiser, ruling Germany once again! The French are probably going to request for some German land, which we have no choice but to grant them."

The next day

- Dear soldiers and officers, today we will make history! It's going to be the first time for many reaching the German mainland! With your help, tonight we can liberate Dresden! It's only 30 kilometers away and the Nazi resistance is almost nonexistent.

(crowd cheer)

- Listen everybody, we will attack the city from two sides. One army group would attack Freiberg, which should look like our main objective. We expect troops from Leipzig and Dresden to go there. All we need to do is to slow them down! The railway station is the goal, not the capture of the city.

(clears throat)

- The railway station is in the south of the city, it will be among the first buildings we come in contact with! While all of this is ongoing, I will command the second army group, which would take Dresden. We will advance along the Elbe River and go northeast until we reach the city or meet a lot of resistance. Once this is achieved, the troops stationed in Freiberg would move 30 kilometers towards Dresden. This will serve as a nice distraction, which means that we can get closer to the city. Got mitt uns!
- Got mitt uns, Kaiser! – shouted everyone.

(soldiers cheer)

30 minutes later

"Reinhardtsdorf-Schöna is the first mainland German village I came in contact with. They were very welcoming and glad to see the Kaiser back. We were cheered on and the women backed bread for our soldiers.

I ordered them to not spend more than 5 minutes celebrating, as we need to advance. In the meantime, I visited the local church. It's a Lutheran Church from the 17th century and it contained many impressive Christian wooden sculptures. I'm surprised that the Nazis hadn't stolen them, just so they can fund their economy.

So far, we haven't met any resistance, I wonder how long this would last."

20 minutes later

"Königstein is a bigger town we just liberated, again we were met not by resistance, but by cheering public, who couldn't wait to see the Kaiser return.

We asked them did the Nazis ever came to this town and they confirmed that they did. It was especially active days ago, when the Sudetenland crisis was ongoing.

They said that this day when they woke up, all the Nazis were gone and appeared to be in a rush. I think they're either going Dresden, or I have no idea. We will be more cautious next."

30 minutes later

"We have reached the city of Pirna. Right now, we're progressing from smaller to bigger cities. Now we actually encounter resistance. The city is on the both banks of the Elbe, so we're getting shelled from the eastern side. The Wehrmacht soldiers on the western side look to have surrendered.

We attacked them and after we shelled each other for a bit, they gave up out of nowhere. After Heidenau, the road to Dresden is clear."

(radio buzz)

- How is the situation on Freiberg, commander?

(radio buzz)

- We encountered little resistance and when fighting actually broke out, the enemy surrendered. They look to be demotivated. The soldiers also appeared to be left without a commander, as they couldn't respond to us effectively.

(explosion)

(pauses)

(radio buzz)

- A shell landed nearby, continue.
- We're ready to advance towards Dresden, under your command.
- I approve, we will be there in 30 minutes, unless there are complications on the frontlines.

(radio buzz)

20 minutes later

- Are we ready to advance towards Heidenau?
- Ja, Kaiser! – the commanders responded.
- We will have two army groups attacking the city. One will go along the railroad and another along the river. The enemy is not using artillery and most likely they haven't adjusted it for this position.
- Correct. Your command has improved. In the beginning your orders mirrored the tactics of the Great War, neglecting the enemy's airplanes and armor advantage.

(silence)

(man rushes to reach both men)

- Commander, Heidenau has surrendered already?
- What?
- Your Majesty, we didn't sent soldiers to the area, we scouted the area and the enemy is waving a white flag.
- Why would they do that?
- I will call Prague and ask for more information regarding the matter.

(man walks away)

(man goes into a tent)

(radio buzz)

- Right now we're in Pirna, 20 kilometers from the Czech borders and 15 from Dresden. We have received news that the army garrisoning Heidenau has surrendered before we have even entered the city. On the way to Dresden, we encountered little resistance and where we did, the enemy surrendered after briefly fighting.
- Your Majesty, Hitler has been shot!
- What? Please repeat.

- Adolf Hitler was shot dead this morning, we have no further information about that. The Republic of France has also entered the war and have occupied the Saarland. The Nazi Government is yet to surrender, so you should continue your advance.
- What are the goals of the French? We were already winning without them! Do they intervene because they want to steal land?
- Possibly. They justified it because of the discoveries at Mauthausen, as well as public pressure.
- What about Mauthausen?
- It is confirmed that it's become a concentration camp, where undesirable, deemed by the Reich, were sent there to be eliminated, but not before they use them as a literal slave labor.
- Gott…
- Yes…

(radio buzz)

(man goes out of tent)

- Commander, the French are also in the war, Hitler is shot dead.
- This explains a lot.

(since)

- What's our next move?
- We start liberating cities and eliminating Nazi resistance. We will be in Berlin by the end of the month! See you at the Brandenburg gate!

2 weeks later

- Gentleman, we have gathered here Strasbourg, where we will discuss the terms of the German surrender. Let us welcome everybody in the room - French President Paul Reynaud.

(people start clapping)

- His Majesty, Kaiser of German people, the leader the German Empire in Exile, Wilhelm III.

(people applaud)

- The defender of Czechoslovak freedom and territorial integrity, President of the Federation of Central Europe, Edvard Beneš.

(people cheer loudly)

- The defender of Austrian freedom, the first pray of the Nazi expansionist policy, Benito Mussolini.

(people applaud slowly)

- And finally, we have the Polish President Ignacy Mościcki, who has returned Danzig to his glorious nation.

(cheer)

- Now, let us first discuss the most pressing issue. Do we agree that Kaiser Wilhelm III should be returned to the throne of Germany, with the German state becoming a constitutional monarchy.
- I approve of that. – said Benito Mussolini.
- I'm in favor. – added Edvard Beneš.
- Yes, but under conditions! – said Paul Reynaud.
- We will agree to that, but we would want guarantees from the new Kaiser. – said Ignacy Mościcki.
- What kind of guarantees are you looking towards?
- Poland wants to keep the free city of Danzig and the territory it has gained from the German Empire after the end of the Great War. In exchange of Kaiser supporting our annexation of Danzig, a non-aggression pact, and promises not to claim Polish lands, we can come to an agreement.
- The German Empire can promise this to the Polish Republic!

(both men shake hands)

- Then, Poland is in favor of this motion.

(everybody nods)

- Your Excellency, President Paul Reynaud, under what conditions will you accept Kaiser Wilhelm III to establish a monarchy in Germany?

(clears throat)

- France should directly annex the Saarland, and the Versailles peace treaty should be applied to the German Empire. This means that the Rhineland would get demilitarized once again, with the army count of the German Imperial Army being limited to 100,000 soldiers.
- I object!
- This is absurd.
- No, this cannot work out!

(discontent among the people in the room)

- Your Excellency, President Paul Reynaud, I don't think that we can accept this. I was in Paris about a month ago and I met you to discuss a possible French intervention, and you declined. The German Empire is not the Weimar Republic or the German Reich, we're a completely new state and should be threated as such. I'm happy to sign a treaty of friendship with you, but we cannot have Versailles put upon Germany.
- And why not?
- Because Czechoslovakia could in theory have a million men and invade us. Same with Poland or even France. We need to become the protectors of Central Europe from Bolshevism and communist revolutions. I propose to get rid of the army limit. In return, we will guarantee the independence of Poland from the ever-growing Soviet aggression and their communist influence abroad.
- And Kaiser, what about the Saarland and the Rhineland?
- France deserves the Saarland, as they did declare war and occupy it. This helped us end this conflict quicker and saved thousands of lives. This doesn't mean that they should demilitarize the Rhineland. We're happy to sign guarantees, but no such heavy restrictions should be placed upon our state. I believe quite the opposite. If we apply Versailles again to Germany, this time the communists will rise and do what the Nazis tried to do, which is to undo the treaty's harm. Applying the same treaty and expecting a different outcome isn't going to work.

- Italy agrees.
- Poland too!

(people nod)

(silence)

- France will agree, but we would need many guarantees in return. You need to renounce your claims on Malmendy-Eupen and promise not to intervene in the Benelux in any way, shape or form.
- We can work with that, the German Empire agrees.
- Good, we're making some real progress. Finally, we have the topic of Austria, what should happen to them? Austrian Burgenland is held by the Hungarians, so we cannot discuss the future of that territory right now, without Hungarian representation.
- Italy, suggest they remain an Italian protectorate and are released as an independent state.
- France suggests the same and supports Italy.
- The German Empire prefers Austria to join the Federation of Central Europe, and that Italy should be compensated elsewhere.
- What?
- What if the Italians gain their claimed parts of Yugoslavia, as per the Treaty of London, instead of a protectorate over Austria.
- I wouldn't be opposed to that! – Said Mussolini.
- The German Empire thinks that the rise of the Nazis happened because of an unfair peace treaty. We should honor Italy's participation accordingly in the Great War, even though they fought against my father.
- And how do we force Yugoslavia to redraw their borders and lose land?
- I suggest that France and Czechoslovakia just pull out their guarantees on the nation.
- We can do that, but only if you take just the territories promised to your country in 1915.
- I promise to do that! – Said Mussolini.

(silence)

- There is only one small problem. If I go out of this peace deal without having gained any territory, Italy is going to rebel, and a civil war can

follow. If we want a stable Apennine Peninsula, you need to agree that the Kingdom of Italy should also establish a protectorate over Albania, with whom we are close allies and part of the Rome Protocols.
- We consent to that.

(men shake hands)

- Well, I believe we have made great progress and hopefully this will lead us to a more stable and prosperous Europe! Thank you all for attending!

What's the equivalent of the Eiffel Tower in Germany?

- Attention everyone! The Kaiser is back!

(people cheer)

- After the fall of the Nazi regime and the Weimar Republic, we finally have a leadership that has historically proven to be very stable! It should have continued this way, hadn't it been for France and the United Kingdom, who forced the royal family out, and replaced them with a dysfunctional democracy. Let this be a new age for Germany! Long live Kaiser! Long live the German Empire!
- Long like Kaiser! – the people shouted back!

Back in German East Africa

(man turns on radio)

"Kaiser Wilhelm III has officially become the monarch of the German Empire. He will rule under a constitutional monarchy, so many political parties have returned to Germany.

Kaiser has also promised the people of East Africa independence and an official alliance. Kaiser Wilhelm III wants the East African colonies to vote on whether they want to remain German or achieve their independence.

He said that he hopes if they go the independence path, that the two nations will not separate and can work closely together, or maybe create an unlikely alliance of equals. Tomorrow, the people of East Africa will vote regarding their future."

- So, who are we voting for?
- As much as I like Kaiser, he will focus on ruling Germany, not us. He will probably send a representative, who will do a poor job. I say we secure

- our independence and cooperate with him. This way, we can choose who comes to govern us, not him.
- Strong words, but don't you think he has done much for this nation?
- He has! Africa has never been so prosperous! It was only because of him. Undoubtedly, we're the strongest African country. We should secure our independence and then force the colonizers to do the same to their colonies!
- Don't you think this would get us invaded?
- We're as strong as an European country, so we can resist. We deserve our place in the world.
- Let's not get ahead of ourselves and join the German Commonwealth after we get independence.
- Agreed.
- I think that most of the population would vote for that option too. This is out of respect for Kaiser, but also for desire for independence.

4 days later

(man reads newspaper)

"East Africa has voted to become an independent country, with a federation being established. Right now, all of the East African colony would become independent at once. It includes many nationalities, so a federation is the only possible way to avoid further break up, and to secure the prosperity of the region.

Either way, the East African people hold respect for Kaiser and wish to join the German Commonwealth, which is an economic and military alliance."

- Well, there goes our colony.
- They did deserve it, after all, many natives died for you, your Majesty, to return.
- I still think they're ungrateful.

(silence)

- Well... they voted for it. What are we going to do next?

- Do you know what's the German equivalent of the Eiffel tower?
- I don't, are there any?
- Exactly! There isn't! How come such a great nation with such great people doesn't have something spectacular to show for it?
- What are you suggesting?
- I think we should build a monument of myself in Berlin, overlooking the Austrian Alps, portraying me as a hero! I want it to be made out of bronze, but to have silver and gold features. I want it to be bigger and greater than the Statue of Liberty! The world must know that Kaiser has returned and how great the German people are!
- This is very ambitious, your Majesty, but I will do my best to fulfil this request.
- You better hurry up! I want to see it while I'm alive!
- Yes, your Majesty! Your word is the law!

The next day

(man lights cigar)

- I want to meet the leaders of the Baltic states and offer them a deal.
- What is it about?
- Don't ask too many questions!
- Of course, I'm sorry, your Majesty!

10 minutes later

- Your Majesty, I have secured a meeting in Riga for tomorrow morning. I will give you more details later.
- Whatever. You're free to go now.

(door opens door closes)

The next day

- Dear Baltic brothers. I have gathered you here in one of the most beautiful cities I have ever been in. As you may know, I have already promised Poland protection against the Soviet Union, in return of them supporting my rule over Germany.

(clears throat)

- Now, I think that the Baltic nations cannot resist the Soviet Union on their own. The Soviets have clearly shown their ambitions to restore the borders of the former Russian Empire, but not us, we're better than that. I come here with an offer, one that if I were you I'd accept. The German Empire is willing to extend their guarantees to the Baltics, but not for free.
- So, what do you want in return?
- I think it's only fair to say that we want Memel back from Lithuania. In compensation for that, we will negotiate with the Poles, who are also our allies, that they return Wilno to Lithuania.
- Hm...

(man nods head slowly)

- In addition to that offer, I request the lease of the whole Estonian island of Saaremaa. It will officially remain within the boundaries of your nation, but we request it, so we can build military bases there. Does it make sense? It's all to guarantee that a German task force can respond quickly to a possible Soviet Invasion. If we don't do these border changes, we have no reason to protect you and even if we did, German troops wouldn't reach you in time. Do you all consent to that?
- I'm in favor. - said Antanas Smetona.
- Latvia agrees.

(pause)

- Estonia will also agree.
- Good.

(men shake hands)

- I promise you, this will lead to a better future.

- What are the terms of the lease of Saaremaa?
- Once the Soviet Union has seized to exist, it would be returned to Estonia. Until then, we will need it.
- Sounds a bit harsh. – everybody agreed.
- Well, these are my terms. I would say that your nation seizing to exist is even more harsh!

(silence)

- Well, it was good talking to you, but I have better things to do back home. My people will send you the paperwork.

(door opens, door closes)

- What a jerk!
- I heard he wasn't like this, but ruling Germany changed him.
- It's all about participating in that war.
- Look what a war can do to you!

2 days later, back in Germany

- Kaiser, the Kingdom of Italy has just invaded Yugoslavia.
- And? This is what we agreed to.

(silence)

- They request weapons, as they helped you out, they hope you can help them out too!
- We didn't agree to this, deny their request.
- I understand.

(door opens, door closes)

(man reads newspaper)

"Today, the Kingdom of Italy has crossed into the territory of the Kingdom of Yugoslavia, without prior warning. The Italians are attacking from three fronts. One from the northernmost front in Slovenia, one from the Italian port city in Zara, and another from Italian-controlled Albania.

Rumors have spread that the Tsardom of Bulgaria were promised Macedonia if they intervene on the Italian side, but so far, this has been rejected by the Tsar.

The Prince Regent Paul Karađorđević has taken drastic measures to stop this advance from happening. All the communists and socialists in the country, which prior to that were suppressed, were allowed to exist. This has created a far more united Yugoslavia against the foreign invaders.

The Soviet Union is looking like they would support the socialists in Yugoslavia, which would perhaps secure their territorial integrity. Soviet aid fails to reach Yugoslavia, as Italy controls the sea, and no bordering country would allow the socialist aid to pass through.

Stalin is eying up the Kingdom of Romania, as they claim Bessarabia from the country, but also to secure an ally, so the aid can reach Yugoslavia. These times are truly turbulent, and anything can happen!"

- Ha! These morons are fighting over nothing. Germany is not ready for a war, but if the Baltics are attacked... well... too bad for them! We have already secured our gains.

Life is good! I feel good!

- The people of the German Empire, it is I, your beloved Kaiser, chosen by God himself to rule you, want to celebrate the completion of the construction of a monument we shall all remember. A monument so large it would dwarf the Eiffel Tower and the Statue of Liberty, because the German people are the strongest and have been through a lot, am I right?

(crowd cheers)

- Order has officially been restored in the German Empire. All Nazis have been purged out of the public space. What we found at Mauthausen is the greatest disaster that has ever happened to the German people, and it deserves a monument, just not yet!

(crowd cheers)

- Now, my beloved people, I present to you the monument of myself!

(pulls down tarp)

(crowd gasps)

- This marvel of a construction was achieved in only 3 months, with the aid of the smartest people in Germany, and subsequently the whole world! Let this remind you of the German greatness, of Kaiser's greatness, of the bravery and the lives lost! We must honor everyone who died!

(man walks off stage)

- So, Jacob, we made it! – said a stranger in the crowd to his friend.
- Damn right, Hans! See, life is worth living after all.
- Well, we're no longer millionaires, which I will miss.

(laughter)

- Let's go out and drink one, you know, for the victory.

- I wish I could, let's go out tomorrow! I have to help Mila with the kids.
- Ha! Who beat you in the head to have 4 daughters?

(laughter)

- Come at the usual place tomorrow after work!
- I will!

(man walks away)

20 minutes later

- Honey, I'm home!
- You're not late this time, Hans.
- I'm not! I thought I would, but I went early and got to see the Kaiser. He saved us!
- I made dinner, come and sit down, you can tell me.
- Daddy, you're home – Hans' daughter approached him.
- Hey little one!
- Daddy, daddy!

(3 other blonde children approach their father)

- Hi babies, daddy is home!

(babies cheer)

- Go and see what mama is doing and let daddy undress.
- Yes, mama! – the kids followed their mother to the kitchen.

Minutes later

- Dinner's ready!
- I'm hungry, are you kids hungry?
- Depends on… what's for dinner?
- Always your favorite sweetheart!
- Yay!

(kids rush to the kitchen)

- Kids, today I managed to see Kaiser!
- Yay, Kaiser! Long live! Right?
- Right!
- What? Did your father teach you this?
- Yes, mommy!

(gives an angry look)

- Clara! Don't bite your sister!
- Let's eat now. We're looking forwards to a great life after this!

Tomorrow morning

(alarm buzz)

(man gets up)

(gets ready for work)

(door opens, door closes)

(cars beep at a busy intersection)

- Hello there! Today I'm not late.
- Great to see you here, but today you're not at work.
- Why? Am I fired?
- No, the Kaiser has decided that today will be a national holiday, as such, government workers will take the day off.
- Gott, he's always so humble!
- He is great. Now have a good end to the day. Jacob also came early and told me to let you know the place. He said you know where.
- I would have guessed, Danke!
- Tschüss

(man waves for goodbye)

Minutes later

- Ha! I was instructed to find you here!
- And I knew you would come early, I already ordered you beer.

(man passes glass to another man)

- So, Kaiser is being humble again? A national holiday? And we still get paid? He is truly the best!
- He is!

(both men sip from the glass with beer)

- So, Hans, do you miss home?
- No, what about you?
- Why not?
- Now it's part of France, so it's no longer home. I also didn't enjoy working in the steel factory. Here in Berlin, we have more opportunity, and Kaiser is making it good for everybody!
- We did grow up there, right?
- It doesn't matter. If we stayed, we would still work in the steel factory and may have to learn to speak French, can you imagine?

(man lights a cigarette)

- Hey, can I borrow one?
- Thought you quit them.
- Someday I will.
- Here.

(man gives a cigarette to his friend)

- Had we remained in Saarbrücken, I bet I wouldn't be able to feed my 4 daughters.
- The French aren't that bad.
- You think so? Because I think they're the worst!
- You know what, Hans, ever since we have moved here and Kaiser is back, you're a completely different person. I have noticed you love life more; you love to work more…

- And love Kaiser!
- Correct.
- Do you think that Kaiser should return Saarland to the Germans, or let the French have it?
- You know what, Jacob, I'm done with warfare. For as long as I'm alive, I don't want Germany to join any wars.
- Good point, me too! Let's drink with that!

(glasses bang against each other)

(both men drink beer)

3 hours later

"On the way home I'm just realizing how much I have really changed and improved. Kaiser really did save me and my family... and also my work. Without him, nothing that I have done would be possible, ever.

The Weimar Republic was the biggest disaster. It's soon going to be 15 years since I killed this person at the steel factory. Nobody knows, just me. It's such a big pressure for me to keep it up, but I have to.

I was scared during the Nazi regime, but I complied and was spared any hardships. Their rule didn't last long either way. Under a Kaiser I was raised and under a Kaiser I feel myself. I'm so happy he is back! Long live Kaiser!"

Revolution!

(man turns on radio)

"The war in the Balkans intensifies. The Kingdom of Romania has declared general mobilization and intent to protect Bessarabia from the Soviet Union.

On the other hand, the Kingdom of Yugoslavia is holding and has lost minor territories. All of Slovenia has been lost, as well as parts of the historical provinces of Kosovo and Macedonia.

The Kingdom of Italy has officially blocked all Yugoslav ports, so a famine is on its way, especially in Bosnia, which is the poorest region of the Kingdom. The people there are radicalized, and communist ideas are spreading.

The Kingdom of Greece is helping their historical ally of Serbia, which is now Yugoslavia. Greek ports are receiving supplies, which are then transported to Belgrade by train. The Kingdom of Italy has threatened with war if this doesn't seize immediately, but the Greeks are resisting this move and are calling Mussolini's bluff.

This is why in the following days, we can expect a lot of action in the province of Macedonia. We can predict that the Italians would want to cut the supply flowing from Greece, to Belgrade..."

(loud bang on door)

- Kaiser, we have an urgent problem!

(door opens, door closes)

- Oh, what is up now, can't you see that I'm busy?
- Your Majesty, we're in big trouble!
- How come?
- Since you allowed partial democracy in the country, the politicians that you allowed have done some digging and have found something that they shouldn't have.
- Such as?

- They saw that we made Versailles worse on purpose, so a tyrannical government would rise in Germany, and you can come and save the people from it, while also becoming Kaiser in the process.

(glass drops, it breaks)

(silence)

- Get out.

(silence)

- Out!

(door opens, door closes)

(man writes on paper)

"No matter how good you are, if you do only one mistake, the people are only going to remember you for this. I'm not going to go down in history as the man who saved the Germans from the Nazis and their extermination camps, but as the one who allowed for it to happen.

I want to let the people know that I did what was right. This move was done because of the incompetence of the Weimar Republic, which was supposed to replace us..."

(man lights a cigar)

- My final one?

(smiles)

(silence)

(puffs on cigar)

(continues writing)

"I am not the one who allowed the Nazis to rise, but France and Britain and their damn Versailles treaty! If they allowed us to remain in power, but my father abdicated in my favor, all would be successful. It wasn't me, I'm not the enemy, but the people's hate would be directed against me.

I hope that I am forgiven by my people, but I really doubt that. After all I had done as Kaiser in East Africa and now the mainland too, I get to stop being one because of something like this. Many people will not understand, but I had to do it!

My son will now inherit my titles, I still hope that he does better than me. The people will hate me, but the German Empire will go on!

I don't consider it possible for me to blackmail the politicians that have found these documents, nor do I want to. They know that they will gain more power if I give them concessions and they keep it a secret.

In the long run, this would only hurt the German Empire, which would hurt me the most! If my fate is to abdicate, I can still go back to East Africa, but I don't want to run anymore. The German Empire is my purpose and anything else that I do is a life not worth living. I hope after my death, the people remember me for what I am, with something good. The last thing I want to happen to me is be remembered like Napoleon III. I'm no Napoleon III, I'm Wilhelm III."

(crowd booing from outside)

- You made us suffer for 15 years so you can return!
- You ruined it all!

(crowd screaming dissatisfied)

- I guess this is how they will remember me...

(door bangs)

- Your Majesty, quickly you have to escape! The people have broken through, and they want to take you with them.

(silence)

(sign)

- Let them.
- What?

(silence)

- You heard me, Karl, let them. I'm afraid I'm tired of running. They want revenge, let them have it!
- No, your Majesty, you have gone insane!
- I have not. I don't any more German blood to be spilled. Tell the guards to stop resisting them, somebody may get hurt.

"The last thing I want to do is to hurt the German people…"

(silence)

- Now! – scream Kaiser Wilhelm.
- Yes, your Majesty!

(door opens, door closes)

(silence)

(man relights cigar)

(looks through the window)

- Traitor!
- You're worse than Hitler!
- Germany is going to be better without you!
- Go back to Africa, we don't want you here!
- Your return was a mistake!

"On and so on, are they right? Maybe. I just know I had to do what I had to do. They will hate me, but my son will hopefully learn from my mistakes and build a better German Empire. I'm too tired to rule a country either way."

(door slams)

- There he is!
- Get him!

(crowd pulls the man away from the window)

(they carry him downstairs)

- We got him! He's ours!
- Oh, now you will learn what it's like to live under Nazism, which you created!

(mob starts beating a man)

- Hey! Stop!
- Police! Stop what you're doing!

(the police save the man of being beaten to death)

- Back off, everyone!
- Hey, don't save him!
- Yeah, he deserves it!
- We suffered way worse!

(police shoots gun into the air)

- I will repeat, back off!

(police carries the man into a car)

(they drive away)

1 hour later

(door cell opens)

- Your Majesty, this is Johann Kundt, I will be your defense.
- Defense?
- The people have decided they want to put you on trail for the crimes against the German people you have committed.
- Crimes, what crimes? I didn't break any law.
- No, you didn't. But they want to sue you for high-treason and get you executed.

(silence)

- If that were to happen, can you make sure that my son takes over after I die?
- I cannot assure you this, your Majesty. I don't have the power for such a thing, I'm simply a lawyer. You're asking the wrong person, I will tell you that much.
- How is the situation looking?
- Do you want the real answer or what you want to hear?
- I want a cigar or something to drink, do you have any?
- No, your majesty, I'm afraid not.
- Make sure to bring some next time.
- There is not going be a next time, everything will happen right now. After an hour you would be in front of the judges.

(silence)

- So, what did you say the situation was.
- Odds are not looking good, I will tell you that much. The people are radicalized and believe the lies they heard, most of which are not true. I have heard some people claim that you have started the war between the Kingdom of Italy and the Kingdom of Yugoslavia.
- Depends how you look at it.
- So, is it true?

(silence)

- After the war, I suggested that the Italians gain something from the Kingdom of Yugoslavia and the Albanian Kingdom, instead of reestablishing their protectorate over the Austrian Federation. Czechoslovakia also participated in the war but had nothing to gain territorially. I knew they would most likely request Silesia, Upper and Lower Lusatia, or something like that. I was not willing to give up any land, so I gave Austria to them.

(man nods head)

- But I didn't start any wars. The Kingdom of Italy is the one who was betrayed after the end of the Great War. They promised they would take simply what is theirs and no more.

(pauses)

- Herr Kundt, let me tell you, this is all part of the plan of the Allies! They want to get rid of me, this is it. I know it.
- How come?
- What is going to happen after I die, can you take a guess?
- I really cannot, your Majesty, I'm sorry.
- Let me tell you my version. The politicians that betrayed me would be seen as heroes and seize power, turning Germany democratic again. This is all the Allies want, this is why they didn't object much to me returning to power!
- But we cannot prove it, we need to present concrete proof that this has happened in front of the court.
- How can we collect all the proof we need for me to get to live for another day in just an hour? They have been planning this for months maybe. Odds are against me.
- It's hard, I would agree, but I would try my best to save you. I fear that your death would start a civil war! You have people that love you with their lives and are willing to forgive, and others that hate you with a passion, who will never forgive.
- Present this to the judge.
- What?
- What you just said.
- That it would start a civil war?
- Correct!

(pause)

- Well, this may be our strongest case we can present. I will try my best to make sure that you live, maybe under house arrest, but alive. Then the people would have time to reconsider their decisions.
- Or I can become elected as President later, if I have enough domestic support.

- You're right, your Majesty! I'm optimistic we can secure a deal!

(pauses)

- These bastards!

(silence)

- They tricked me.

10 minutes later

(man approaches the jail cell)

- Gentlemen, it's time! Put on this suit and follow me.
- Herr Kundt, do you think that the people are going to be more sympathetic if I wear civilian clothes than a suit?
- I think so, once I tried it and it works, but I don't guarantee it.
- Worth the try, am I right?

(silence)

- Well, we're ready to leave,
- Follow me!

(crowd booing)

- Traitor!
- Hope they chop your head off!
- We don't want you, nor your son!
- Long live democracy!

(all men enter a vehicle)

- In 5 minutes, we would arrive in Justizpalast. The Palace of Justice. Your courtroom is number 600. If you can't find it, it's situated in the east of the palace.
- Danke. At least we know where we're going, am I right your Majesty?

(silence)

- It's understandable he doesn't want to speak. Kaiser, you better hope this guy with you is the best lawyer in all of Germany... no in all across the world! Ha.
- Can we just enjoy the silence until we arrive? I assume there's going to be very loud.

(silence)

"Well, here goes my fate and it's not even in my hands. You can do a hundred positive and kind acts, but the people will remember you for the one you failed at. What a shameful world we live in..."

- Hey, Herr Kundt, I want to ask you something. You should go to my palace after that, no matter what happens, and try to find Karl.
- Karl who?
- Don't worry about it, you will find him. Just ask him to publish all the papers, journals, and everything I've got. This is of urgent importance to me.
- I will, Kaiser, I promise.
- I need another promise.
- Yes?
- I never got to say goodbye to my wife. Do you have a pen and paper?
- Let me see.

(man searches through his pockets)

- Here, take this.

(man writes on the back seat)

"Dear Cecilie Auguste Marie, I'm writing to express to you that I'm sorry for the loss you're about to receive. Take care of the children and know that I will always love you!"

- Here, hand this to her when you get the chance to see her! This is the final thing I will request you do for me!
- Of course, your Majesty, I promise!

(pauses)

- Gentlemen, we've arrived. Brace yourself, a big crowd has formed.

(car door opens)

- Traitor!
- The Germans will never miss you!
- You're a puppet of Mussolini!
- You started the war in Yugoslavia!
- I hope you will die here!

(security pushes the men away)

- Your Majesty, dear Kaiser, I'm Hans Schneider, I'm your biggest supporter. Don't lose hope, I believe you made Germany great and you will continue to rule it!
- I appreciate that, Hans, will remember your name.

(both men shake hands)

- I cannot live a life not under the German Empire, and I cannot raise my kids in a democratic environment. I wish you all the best! Many of us support you!
- Danke, Hans!
- Good luck!

(man enters into the building)

- Head to the east, up the stairs, courtroom number 600, remember?
- We do!
- Good luck, Kaiser!

(men walk towards the entrance)

- Room 600, there it is.
- Well, here goes nothing.

(door opens, door closes.)

- Everybody stands up!

(camera lens shutter)

- Friedrich Wilhelm Victor August Ernst, you have been accused of high treason and we have many evidence that you have made Versailles harsher for the German people, so you can guarantee a rise of a tyrannical state. We also know that you promised the Italians the Kingdom of Yugoslavia, so you're the reason this war has happened. On top of all that, the Soviet Union is preparing to enter the Kingdom of Romania, so they can reach Yugoslavia. This can quickly spiral out of control and start a world war. All because of your fault and your greed for power! Had you accepted your fate, we wouldn't be here right now. You were defeated sooner or later, but it took you 20 years to get here. There was no need to escape to East Africa and delay your fate. What do you have to say in your defense?
- Herr Kundt.
- The Kaiser admits that he is guilty, but I urge you not to force him the death penalty. Outside of the Palace of Justice, there are not only people who hate Kaiser, but also people who love him and support him. If Kaiser is killed, this would radicalize them. A civil war in Germany is imminent.
- Your Majesty, we shouldn't forget that your moves to make Versailles harsher did pave the way for the rise of Adolf Hitler, his Nazi party, and the German Reich. These people did some unimaginable acts of horror. You allowed this to happen, you set up the conditions to that! Adolf Hitler was assassinated, so he couldn't get a trial, but you can. I hereby charge you with the crimes against humanity and the acts done in the extermination camp, as you allowed them to happen. Had you just accepted your fate, the German people would be living under democracy, but you decided to make it harsher for everyone. You better hope that the Soviet Union doesn't invade the Kingdom of Romania, so it wouldn't start another massive global war, just because of your selfishness and greed of power. I sentence you to death by handing.

(the wooden hammer strikes the podium)

(silence)

…

(crowd stands up and applauds)

(people cheer)

(a person opened a nearby window)

- People! The Kaiser will be hanged!
- Finally!
- He deserves it!
- Long live democracy!
- Long live the German freedom!

(a man in the crowd thought to himself)

"Kaiser is getting hanged. Whan an unfair world... they set him up, he just arrived... This is no fair trial."

The next day

- Kaiser Wilhelm III, Friedrich Wilhelm Victor August Ernst, born on the 6th of May 1882. Do you have any last words.
- Gott mit uns!

(chair breaks)

(man hangs on the rope)

(his neck breaks)

(silence)

Thank you for reading!

I acknowledge the inconsistency of historical events and it being not accurate by any means, but it's not supposed to be one. I prioritized entertainment and if you're reading this, I guess I have done a good enough job.

To me, content that contains too much historical accuracy is dull, because each small change needs to be justified for longer, in turn making the whole thing longer and more boring.

If you liked what you have read so far, you can check out my social media, so you can get in contact with me for whatever reason. Thank you again for reading, really appreciate that!

Where to find the author?

I, Rewriting History, have a YouTube channel where I upload alternate history scenarios, just like this one. You can find me by searching "Rewriting History" on YouTube, or by going to this link:

https://www.youtube.com/@rewriting-history/

If you want to support me further, you can subscribe to my Patreon. If this book release goes well, I would like to do more and improve my skillset. I would still need to pay the bills, so any support on Patreon goes to that. Here is the link for that:

https://www.patreon.com/RewritingHistory/membership

Email: ouuteu@gmail.com

Printed in Great Britain
by Amazon